DYSTOPIAN

FALLS

The Fence Book III

By C.G. Buswell

Copyright © C.G. BUSWELL LTD 2024
All Rights Reserved.

www.cgbuswell.com

This is a work of fiction, and any character that bears a resemblance to anyone living or dead is a coincidence. The author imagines the events and places and bears no similarities to actual events or places.

For Jonny. Thank you for the coffee, cakes, laughter, and fellowship.

Chapter 1	1
Chapter 2	9
Chapter 3	16
Chapter 4	27
Chapter 5	33
Chapter 6	40
Chapter 7	44
Chapter 8	51
Chapter 9	61
Chapter 10	66
Chapter 11	72
Chapter 12	78
Chapter 13	88
Chapter 14	100
Chapter 15	111
Chapter 16	123
Chapter 17	126
Chapter 18	131
Chapter 19	137
Chapter 20	142
Chapter 21	146
Chapter 22	152
Chapter 23	158
Chapter 24	165
Chapter 25	169

Chapter 26	176
Chapter 27	180
Chapter 28	185
Chapter 29	190
Chapter 30	195
Chapter 31	202
Chapter 32	209
Chapter 33	216
Chapter 34	228
Chapter 35	235
Chapter 36	240
Chapter 37	245
Chapter 38	252
Chapter 39	255
Chapter 40	261
Chapter 41	265
Chapter 42	273
Chapter 43	277
Chapter 44	281
Author's Note	284

Chapter 1

The youth snapped his head back, bloodied hands grasping at his black hoodie. He flung the fabric back. It bounced to rest between his shoulder blades. As he craned his neck to emit a howl, several 7.62mm rounds tore into his neck, severing his head. His body twisted and cavorted from the impact from the L7A2 General Purpose Machine Gun. The violent movement unfurled his hood, and his head was flung into it like a basketball player slamming home a reverse dunk. The teenager's red eyes dimmed. His body dropped to the concrete skatepark boundary floor, landing on top of his victim, a desperate mother looking for her lost child. They had found each other. Mother and child were now reunited in death. She'd ventured into Bellfield Park after weeks barricaded at home a few streets away in her Banchory home. The two bodies slid down the flat bank of the ramp's bowl, a thick red slime tracing their route to the shallow end. The couple thudded into a lone skateboard, and it rolled its lonely way along the grey course and came to rest by the bloated corpse of a small girl. Infected victims from the Russian chemical air attack had fed on her throat, exposing sinews.

Crows in the nearby trees had eaten greedily upon her, stripping her of clothing in their fervent search for flesh.

Up the hill, parked on the pavement by the main road into this Aberdeenshire town, a battered Land Rover was parked. Through the grey and white smoke from the mighty weapon, two figures, dressed in military multi-terrain pattern combat uniforms, were hunched over a huge black gun. It was mounted on a tripod and swivelled as the GPMG operator aimed down the sights. The butt was nestled tight into the right shoulder of the man and his left hand was on the thick black butt, like he was cuddling a lover. Beside him, a small, thinner, almost emaciated figure was grinning as she fed the link belt containing one hundred of the deadly bullets. The rapid fire was making its way through her gloves quickly, like a grocery checkout assistant at Aldi.

'Fuck me!' shouted Imogen Pritchard above the blasts of the deadly firepower. 'Did you see that head? What a catch!' She turned to her partner and beamed a toothless grin.

Ignoring her, Flight Sergeant Jason Harper continued his short, aimed bursts. Below them, a man in tattered clothing was sniffing around the recently killed, like a dog on a deer carcass. He threw his arms up, as if flapping, as three of the rounds from the disintegrating link belt burst through his chest and exited from his back. A ragged hole the size of a toddler's football burst through the back of his shirt, stripping the fabric from his torso as it continued its trajectory.

A guttural wail erupted from Jason's mouth, coming from deep within his soul. Springing from the machine gun, tears still in his eyes, Jason left the weapon to turn on the free-swinging mount. He scrambled over the side of the Land Rover and puked on the main road into Banchory.

'You'll have to get out of that habit one day, Cowboy,' mocked Imo as she clipped another link belt into place. She slammed home the weapon's feed tray lid, thumping it into place with her fist. The civilian looked across to her forced upon military companion. He should have been taking the lead in this mission to rescue anyone not infected. Shrugging, she pulled back the silver-edged, round cocking handle. Ramming it as far back as she could, she then allowed it to return to the forward position as it fed in a fresh round. Rolling her eyes, she sidled across the Land Rover, kicking aside a pile of spent brass bullet casings. She flicked the link belt over the left side of the vehicle so it went rigid and would self-feed. Aiming at a woman, red-eyed and snarling as she ran up the grass bank towards them, Imo gently pulled the trigger. Several bursts of fire took out the woman's legs, ripping bone and flesh just below her kneecaps. She fell flat on her face, eating grass as she roared. Imogen was flung back during this rapid fire, the recoil forcing her to the back of the Land Rover. She landed on Sabre's blankets, their German Shepherd dog whined as it cushioned her fall.

Jason, climbing back on the vehicle, wiping his mouth with the back of his sleeve, roared with laughter. 'Serves you right. I told you not all weapons are like Call of Duty. You can't learn everything from a computer game or from prison. Top marks on the reload, though. I taught you well.'

Imo winced as he brought up her incarceration spells for drug offences and stealing over the years. Then she gave a scowl as she rubbed her hip. Sabre was a big dog and on the lean side. She tickled his ear and heard Jason whip out his Glock 19 from his holster.

He drew the pistol into the classic firing stance, one foot slightly forward than the other, arms out straight. He fired one shot. Straight into the forehead of the infected woman who was crawling through the wooden fence they were parked by. She had trailed a leg, as she had moved, hanging by her tendons at an awkward angle. It looked like an oversized chicken wing. The heavy-calibre rounds had shorn the other lower leg clean off.

'You missed her. The recoil made you swing low. Normally it causes the gunner to hit higher, but you aren't as tall as most in my regiment.'

'Bollocks to your Royal Air Force Regiment. It's not like you're a proper army, is it?' she teased. 'What's with the roaring and tears? Pippa?'

Jason shook his head vehemently. 'Not just her. I promised I'd never fire something like that again.'

'A GPMG? Is this to do with what the colonel keeps bringing up? The failed mission. I thought you'd be over that by now.' She waved her hand about as she stood up. 'What with all the killing we've done recently?'

He wrinkled his nose. 'The cordite smell is stronger with this weapon. I couldn't shoot that woman in Yemen.'

Flicking her head across to the new corpse, she laughed. 'Looks like you've no trouble in that department, Cowboy.' Taking a step forward, she thumped his back, interrupting his dry retching. 'Best you get something to eat. Besides, we haven't looked in all the kit-bags yet.' Imo thought back to their meeting at the huge fence erected around Aberdeenshire. Built to contain the infected from the testing of the Russian chemical weapon. It caused the population to tear at each other's throats. An ideal weapon designed to decimate and depopulate an area before an invading army's ground troops moved in. Not so good for those uninfected and trapped. Or for those ordered to kill the infected because there was no cure. Military experts thought that the Russian

President would be sanctioning its use in Ukraine. NATO scientists were busy trying to find a cure and vaccination against it. Until then, COBRA had ordered the infected in Aberdeen and the surrounding Shire to be killed. Anyone lucky enough to have survived the attack was to be sent for testing and processing at the Angus border on the A90.

Jason swivelled the GPMG barrel, so it was facing into the town centre. The T-junction with the traffic lights was switched off, along with all the electrics in the Shire and City. Unless ordered by the colonel to be switched back on. He and his staff controlled the power and water supply from their HQ near the fence.

'What did Pippa say to you when I was crying into the phone?' asked Jason, gently.

'I promised to look after you,' stated Imo as Sabre nudged her hand for another ear stroke. She obliged as she thought about her other promise. No need to tell the recently re-enlisted Jason in case his loyalties had switched back to the RAF.

'Thanks. You did, and I know you always will. I doubt the colonel will let us through that fence. We are too valuable to him as a killing team. Banchory isn't the only town he'll send us to.'

She nodded. 'But the bastard re-armed us and supplied us. Those technicians didn't hang around when they bolted the tripod to our Land Rover. Some others threw in the kit-bags. You were still crying when they slapped a handful of combat clothing into our open arms.' She tapped the earpiece wrapped around her ear. 'These will be brilliant for when we get separated. Those people returned to the other side of the fence quick enough. One day we'll get through and you'll be with Pippa again.'

'Sorry.' Jason looked down at the mountain of brass casings.

'Don't be. You've shown me her photo. Pippa is beautiful and glowing. You are blessed to have such a beautiful wife.' She grinned, revealing a toothless mouth again, caused by years of drug abuse and self-neglect. 'You are lucky to have her and to know she and your unborn baby are safe.'

Jason gulped, fighting back tears. As he looked up, he heard the twang of elastic and felt a rush of air pass his left ear, the one without the personal comms attached. A body fell as it was climbing over the side of the vehicle.

Imo kissed her catapult and patted her ammo pouch that was filled with lethal ball bearings. She curtsied, lost her footing amongst the brass casings, and quickly corrected herself. 'You're welcome! Keep your fancy phallic-like weapons. The old ways are the best ways for this old poacher.'

'Ha!' exclaimed Jason, as he reciprocated the back slap. 'I've been trying to think of a nickname for you. Well, one that I can say to your face and not get a kicking! "The Poacher" that's what I'll call you.'

Imo beamed wider. 'I've never had a nickname before, not even in the kid's home or prison. Does this mean we are proper partners now?' she asked eagerly.

Jason drew out his combat knife, aimed it at her, and hurled it. The blade whizzed past her face as she swerved from it, shock upon her face. It squelched into the left eye of a snarling man climbing onto the tailgate of the Land Rover. He thudded to the floor. Jason tipped an imaginary hat at Imo and drawled in his best American accent, like Bob tried on their last mission, in Stonehaven. 'Well, I guess this cowboy just got himself a partner!' He elongated the last word and pronounced the middle letters with a prolonged d. Winking at her; tears now forgotten.

A proud smile erupted on Imo's blood-streaked face, and she struck out a hand and pumped Jason's for all she was worth.

Chapter 2

'Stop fucking around,' barked Colonel Winters into the personal comms of both Imo and Jason. This Special Air Service Commanding Officer could patch into this system from his HQ just south of the fence.

'Fuck off,' drawled Imo, touching her earpiece, not quite used to how it felt. 'You are interrupting a special moment.'

Laughter erupted over the airwaves. 'I like you. I admire your spirit. Now get the fuck out of there and turn left. There are more heat signals coming from the King George V Park.'

Imo and Jason instinctively looked up, hoping for a glimpse of the surveillance drone. They neither heard it nor saw it. The silent data collector would be high amongst the clouds, secretly working away, controlled by the RAF operator at the HQ, maybe even further. They shrugged.

Imo jumped from the Land Rover, stepped onto the nearby body, and yanked out the combat knife. 'Waste not want not,' she yelled back as she cleaned the severed eyeball from the blade on the dead man's shirt. Handing it handle first to Jason as he stepped off the Land Rover, Sabre at his heels, she crouched as he took the blade. She unslung her SA80 rifle from her shoulders and aimed it at the nearby house. Its tall windows gave away that it was a former church, converted into an exclusive home. The lower section of the windowpanes was blood splattered and a red-eyed man in red trousers and a yellow shirt was clawing at the glass. Taking careful aim, Imo released a quick burst. First at him, then at the glass, relishing her clean shot and the explosion of glass. She gave out a loud whoop. 'That's from the fashion police!' she yelled.

'Feel better?' quipped Jason as he drew up his Glock, expecting a release of zombie-like infected from the building. No one else came out, except for the downed man who toppled from the top floor of the former church. His head thudded onto the paving below with a crunch that caused another whoop from Imo.

'Yes!' she yelled. 'That's the furthest I've downed someone with this rifle. Do I get a badge yet?' She tapped her combat tunic in the same arm that Jason had two crossed swords on a patch.

Jason smiled. 'You'll have to do a lot more than that, I'm afraid. The military doesn't give out marksman's badges in lucky bags, you know.'

She scowled. 'I'll drive.' Whistling, pointing to the Land Rover, Imo waited for Sabre to jump back into the vehicle. She didn't pause for Jason before turning the engine over and was already reversing from the pavement as he shut his door. Neither wore seat belts because they wanted to exit the vehicle quickly and all the local police were dead or turned into zombies. The duo had killed several infected officers as they battled their way into Aberdeen several weeks ago.

'Stop fucking around and get on with the mission,' barked Colonel Winters.

Imo swerved between abandoned vehicles and mounted the kerb again. 'Piss off and leave us to get on.'

'You'll do as you are damn well told.'

'Fuck off,' drawled Imo, a smile on her face. She stuck her middle finger up at the CCTV that was on the nearby traffic lights, knowing they would patch an operative into it. Another technician was controlling its power source. She hoped the colonel was watching.

Colonel Winters confirmed this when he teased, 'Both hands on the steering wheel, that's how accidents happen. Now take the first left. The heat sources are coming from the shrubbery behind the skatepark. Work your way through Bellfield Park, then crack on into the larger park.'

'We'll choose our own route. I'm doing your work for you, but I don't work for you.' She tapped Jason's three chevrons and the crown on his rank slide. 'Unless you want to recruit me and pay me. What's the pension scheme like?' She swivelled the vehicle in a car park. The left-hand side was reserved for the patients and staff of a clinic. A wheelchair was parallel to a parked car whose passenger door was wide open. An old lady in a tartan skirt, tan hosiery and a blazer with a white blouse laid motionless, sprawled on the ground. Her skin colour was purple and black from decay. She had died early in the chemical air attack from weeks ago. The wind caused a stench to waft in from Jason's open window where his Glock was poking out. Imo wrinkled her nose.

Ignoring the "No parking, except for staff" signs, Imo drove through, looking for a way to get into the park. Driving round in a circle, she took the next left, mounting the pavement and drove into the skatepark. It made the Land Rover look like an oversized skater. The right-side wheels of the Land Rover crunched over the bodies of the mother and her teenage son, forcing the vehicle to their left. It looked like they were performing a stunt. They reached the junior ramp and took it on two wheels, forcing the Land Rover to raise to one side, causing Sabre to yelp. 'Sorry, boy,' she shouted over her shoulder.

Jason pointed to their right.

Imogen's hands worked furiously on the steering wheel. The vehicle bumped along, righting itself as it squeezed through the back entrance and onto the grass. This well-maintained lawn of Bellfield Park, popular amongst dog walkers and those with toddlers who like to play in the adjacent slides and swings, was kinder on the suspension. She parked it in the middle of the lawn, between rows of sprawling trees that competed to reach the sky. Most had thick trunks that a tree-hugger would struggle to wrap their arms around. 'Fuck the drone. We've a tracker of our own.' She whistled for Sabre as she ran out of the Land Rover and knelt by the bonnet.

Sabre jumped down and ran around the vehicle. Sitting by Imo, licking her ear, tilting his head at the unexpected taste of plastic.

'Don't eat my comms, boy. The colonel will have a hissy fit.' She pointed to the landscaped borders, thick with tall shrubbery, like a cutout island. 'Go find!'

Sabre darted away, diving deep into the plants, pushing them aside with his eager snout, barking deeply as his tail soon disappeared.

'Watch and shoot!' ribbed Jason.

Imo calmly aimed her rifle, steadying her breathing.

A man scurried out from the undergrowth on all fours. His shorts had been shredded over the weeks of his infection. One side of his scrotal sack was poking out and his testicles were swinging fiercely. The singlet had a torn shoulder strap.

It was flapping in the breeze and the garment was covered in blood and earth.

Imogen whistled at him, and the man snapped his head in her direction, revealing red eyes. She grinned lopsidedly as she continued to aim, took a steadying breath, and shot him clean through his balls. They erupted in a splatter with no sign of pain from the castrated man. Another rifle shot cracked through the silent park and he slumped to the floor like an exhausted marathon runner at the finish line ribbon. As he fell, a neat hole spurted blood from his forehead.

'That's got to get me the sharpshooter badge?' she boasted.

Sabre sprinted forward, laid on the grass, and licked around at the red mush.

'I'll give you more than a marksman badge in a minute. You know there are children involved. Now get on with the mission. Secure the area,' ordered Colonel Winters. He shouted the last part of the order, 'And bring them safely to the border.'

Jason nodded to Imo. 'We'll go on foot from here. Is your magazine fully loaded?'

'Of course. I'm not an amateur.' She discretely turned around and deftly reached into an ammo pouch and reloaded her weapon.

'Not after what we've been through.' A shudder ran through his body as he recalled fighting their way through the Buchan area and then into the heart of Aberdeen to find Pippa at her work. It had been in vain. She'd been one of the lucky ones to be helicoptered out to the safety of Dundee. Pointing to the road that split the two parks, Jason holstered his pistol and shouldered his rifle. 'Let's visit the Banchory show.'

'Will there be puppets?' joked Imo.

'No!' barked the Colonel. 'Just you two muppets. If I had my own men at my command, I wouldn't need you two. Damn the Ukrainian invasion.'

'Then shut the fuck up and let us do our work, Gonzo.' Imogen turned to see the grin on Jason's face. 'And don't you dare call me Miss Piggy.' She strode off, clucking for Sabre, who was now licking at the back of the head of the runner. She made a mental note not to allow the dog to give her kisses until its muzzle had a wash.

Chapter 3

Imo whistled through her few remaining teeth. 'Christ on a bike.' Clucking at Sabre, she pointed to her feet. 'Heel, boy, we don't want you in amongst that lot.'

The trio had entered the King George V Park, a grassed area about the size of six football pitches, two abreast. Volunteers had sectioned off areas for the annual Banchory Show. A usually happy time for farmers to showcase their livestock, meet up with friends and let their hair down. There was no gaiety now.

Jason stared at the fallen animals. A mixture of sheep, cows, mighty bulls, horses, ponies, and even a few goats. All were flat on the grass; something had ripped apart throats. The once white sheep, immaculately bathed and groomed for the judges, were crimson-matted. Stomachs were bloated and several had popped with the release of decaying gasses. The nearby crows that roosted upon the trees had fed upon most of the entrails. They watched the two humans and dog like silent mourners at a funeral.

Using the toes of her boot, Imo rolled a white apron wearing man onto his back. Kneeling by the white hat that was trapped under the weight of his body, she quickly frisked his pockets and came out with a fat wallet. In one swift movement, she cleared the cash out and allowed the wallet to fall to the earth. She stowed the purloined money into a pouch of her webbing.

'You'll never be able to spend it. You know that. Right?' sighed Jason. 'Even I know we'll never get through that fence. The colonel will send us wherever he needs us. This mission is a long way off from being over.'

Imo winked at him. 'Old habits. Don't give up yet. We'll get you to Pippa. You'll be there for the birth of your baby.' She patted her pouch. 'I'll buy you the pram.'

Jason pointed around him. 'You can say that, even when we see something like this?' He doubled over, his shoulders heaving.

Imo thumped him on his back. 'Enough of that shit. Let's find those heat sources.' She brought her rifle up and aimed it along each of the corralled sections that had confined the livestock. Other human bodies laid sprawled amongst the dead livestock. Most wore gum boots and gilets, identifying them as farmers. These items of clothing hadn't protected them from the onslaught. Several children, dressed like smaller versions of their parents, lay dead with their mothers and fathers. 'Look the other way, Jason. You don't need to scope out this section. It's clear of the infected. Or it will be in a minute.' Aiming at a trailer, its ramp strewn with hay and straw, she squeezed off a round and shot a teenager running down from the vehicle. It was hitched to a four-by-four, sunk low in the grass. Someone had deflated its tyres. The red-eyed youngster fell onto a sheep. Imo grinned wryly as she thought it looked like he was experimenting with his early sexuality with the livestock. Perhaps it's true what they say about Aberdeenshire sheep farmers, she thought.

Mistaking her smirk, Jason beat her to it. He curtsied and croaked out, 'You're welcome!'

Slipping him a ten-pound note from her bankroll. 'Here you are, hot shot.'

Grinning, despite their surroundings. 'Thanks. For luck.' He pocketed it, hoping the colonel's watchers weren't looking.

She looked deeper into the park. 'I think we are going to need it. Let's get going.'

Leaving behind the overpowering smell of decay, they wove between rows of plastic chairs. Imagining the struggle during the lethal fumes from the enemy aircraft, they stepped over the overturned chairs with caution. Friend would have turned upon friend and family fought each other. Jason carefully stepped over the bodies of men and women who thought they were in for a day of entertainment. In the taped off arena ahead of them young women in tartan skirts that exposed more than their slender legs laid crumpled in heaps. A small drum blew around these Highland dancers, like tumbleweed. Behind them, dressed in full Scottish regalia, despite the late summer sunshine, laid the remains of the Highland Pipes and Drums band.

Imo ran forward and picked up a set of bagpipes, cracking open the fingers that clung to them in death. She stuck the chanter into her mouth and blew for all she was worth. Her cheeks expanded and her face reddened. A faint squeak, like an errant fart in a library, escaped from the pipes. She threw them away as Jason let out a belly laugh. 'Fuck off,' she blurted out.

Replacing his laughter lines with a frown, Jason bit his lip. 'The infected have done what the Russians wanted their new weapon to do. They've killed the survivors and themselves.'

Imo knelt. 'I wouldn't be too sure.' She pointed to a row of open-fronted tents, pop up advertising banners fluttering. From one displaying the latest working dog food came a roaring man wielding a chained dog leash. It was making circles in the air like a lasso.

Jason looked on, mouth agape. Then incredibly, 'They are arming themselves now?'

Looking through her rifle sights, Imo nodded. 'Looks like it. Clever bastards, those Russian scientists. Is that why they take so many civilians back to Mother Russia when they invade countries? As test subjects?'

Jason shuddered. 'It doesn't bear thinking about.' He took two steps forward, shouldered his rifle, and shot the running man through his screaming mouth. Teeth, blood, flesh, and bone shot out behind him. What was left of his head snapped back. His body dropped, and the chain flew into the air and landed on the torn neck of the pipe major.

'Walkies!' retorted Imo, forgiving Jason for stealing her kill.

Jason's eyes lit up. 'Nice one. Walkies. I like it.' Chortling away, it took away his mind from Pippa and the tall fence that separated them.

Colonel Winters doubled up in the control room as if he'd been sucker punched. He slapped the back of the female video operator. 'Brilliant, isn't she? Love her dark humour. She'd have fitted in with all my lads.'

A nervous laugh escaped from her and that of her colleagues. After several weeks of watching the killings in Aberdeen and the surrounding Shire, they finally released their nervous tension.

One operator let out a single tear that gently rolled down his cheek. He'd witnessed the mobile catering truck and kitchen tentage that was delivered in the early hours. They'd moved from cooking their own rations to hot food, freshly prepared by military chefs. They would be here for many more weeks, possibly months. His wedding was officially postponed. He hoped his fiancé would not be tempted back to his former boyfriend again, and he could make him understand.

Sabre nudged the dead dog with his snout, as if to make it play with him. Lying next to him was a woman in red, stained tweeds. Her thick, crook-like stick had not protected her from the onslaught. The German Shepherd's ears pricked up at the whistle from his owner and he left his new plaything and bolted to her.

'Good boy!' exclaimed Imo as she ruffled his thick neck hair. 'We've been told there is a heat source up there and I want you by my side. One of the fuckers is bound to leap at me as I open the door.'

The dog wagged his tail as if understanding every word.

Jason leant slightly forward; weapon raised at forty-five degrees. They were facing a mighty red truck with yellow and black flashes, like flames. It stood on four enormous wheels.

This monster truck formed part of the extreme stunt show. Surrounding it were various motorbikes, their helmeted bikers draped around the metal frames in various death poses. Their visors and leathers had offered no protection from the hordes that had ripped through them.

Imo lifted one motorbike and placed it along the door. She nudged out its kickstand with her toe. The machine stood proudly erect. Springing up onto its seat, her feet wobbling on the leather upholstery, Imo reached up and grabbed the door handle. She prised open the door, then fell. Landing like a cat, instantly grabbing her rifle. Aiming it at the door, she called, 'We'll fire on the count of three.'

A scream echoed from the monster truck's cabin. 'Don't shoot. Don't shoot.' A figure dropped to the ground, crying out as she landed awkwardly.

'You were in there all these weeks?' asked Imo, her eyebrows shooting up.

The young woman rubbed at her left knee, nodding. 'Each time I came out looking for food, a beastly person would try to grab me. Sometimes there were more. They looked dangerous. I've watched all the fighting and killing through the windscreen.'

'Nice vantage point,' admired Jason.

'Shame about the view,' joked Imo, throwing the pale-faced woman a protein bar from one of her pouches. 'What have you been living on?'

'We would go out in the dark and take whatever food and drink we could get from the catering trucks.' She pointed to two white caravan type vehicles with open fronts on either end of the park.

'We?' asked Jason in a low, gentle voice.

'My friend didn't come back one night, when it was her turn to forage.' Between tears, she sobbed, 'We'd always have to run back and jump up into the cabin. People trying to jump up would keep us awake. Their fingernails seemed to dig into the metal and scrape as they fell.'

Imogen crinkled her nose at the stench coming from the unwashed woman. She knew where she had been going to the toilet.

The woman's cheeks went red, as if guessing why this military-looking woman had taken a step back. 'You the army, then? What's been happening?'

Imo sighed, tired of explaining. 'Did you see a plane fly low?'

'Yes, several weeks ago. Soon after, people started attacking each other. We guessed some sort of chemical was released. We had masks on. That was our gimmick this year.

We were dressed like monkeys. Our masks were smelly from overuse. We've toured the UK. We added filters to make them smell nicer.'

'That's what saved your life,' declared Jason. 'Sorry about your friend. Get in your truck and head to Dundee.' He patted one of the thick wheels. 'This will plough through any obstacle along these back roads until you get on the A90.'

She shook her head. Taking a set of keys from her pocket, she threw them against the nearest tyre. They bounced and landed on the grass. 'I always sat in the passenger seat, waved to the crowds, and acted. I've never learned to drive.'

Thinking quickly, Jason asked, 'What's your name?'

'Hazel. My mum always says it matched the colour of my eyes. Will they still be alive? My parents, I mean. They live in Selkirk.' Her eyes squinted in appeal.

Jason nodded. 'Our understanding is the Russians only attacked our area. Aberdeenshire and Aberdeen. It was a single strike.'

Hazel let out a sigh. 'Thank God.'

Spotting the man running towards them, Imo knelt in the shooter's position. His judging white blood-soaked coat flowing in the wind like a matador's cape.

'We've a job to finish here, Hazel. Can you cope with a few more hours in the truck? It'll be safer for you.'

She nodded and let out a squeal as she heard the sharp retort of Imo's rifle. It instinctively drew her gaze to the dropping figure.

Jason patted her shoulder and brought her attention back. He handed her a bottle of fizzy pop from his spare ammo pouch. A stolen treat he'd been saving for later. He added a squished chocolate bar. 'I imagine you are hungry. We'll come back for you once we have secured the area and cook you something hot while we arrange for you to get away safely.'

Hazel nodded vigorously, snatching at the food, biting into the snack with relish.

Jason jumped up onto the motorbike and immediately fell back again. He tried to ignore Imogen's jeering taunts.

Under her breath, she muttered, 'Don't they teach you military boys anything?' Like an agile cat, she sprang up and in one deft movement had the cabin door open. A reeking waft of urine and faeces hit her, and she dropped to the ground, landing in a graceless crouch.

Running under the wheels, Hazel produced a short ladder. She expertly propped it against the open doorframe, scrambled aboard and reeled in the ladder. 'It's usually stored in the sleeping section behind the seats. We rarely use that area when touring. Our own caravans come with us. But I didn't have time to get it onboard when a man in a kilt tried to get in with me. He was snarling and trying to bite me. I kicked him in the face and slammed the door. I locked him out. Fortunately, he and the others couldn't work out how to use the ladder and it eventually fell there.'

'Shut the door,' ordered Jason as he turned from her, bringing his rifle up. He shouted over his shoulder as he let off a quick burst of automatic fire at three women dressed in matching polo shirts. The catering staff wanted their rations back. Only crisps and canned drinks weren't on the menu. They were. 'Lock the door. Only open it for us,' he shouted over his shoulder. He ran forward, switching to single fire, taking more accurate aims as he came to a standstill. He didn't notice Imo crouch by the tyres and rifle through the sporran of a decaying corpse. She cursed as his wallet and valuables slipped through her fingers and knelt in the grass and snatched bank notes into her pouch. She grinned. 'Who says money can't buy you some fun?' as she picked up more of her shiny plunders.

Chapter 4

'Heat sources are coming from the left of you, on the edge of the field,' growled the colonel over their comms.

'Cheers, fella!' grinned Imo as she imagined the highly polished officer bad-mouthing her lack of military etiquette.

Their earpieces stayed silent.

Pointing to a row of various coloured gazebos flapping in the breeze, Jason took the lead.

Stepping over dozens of corpses, Imo knelt several times, as if paying her respects to the fallen. She slipped off watches and rings and rifled through pockets as quickly as one of Fagan's recruits.

'That's enough now!' heeded Jason over his shoulder. 'You'll only weigh yourself down.'

Imo shrugged. She'd had to start her scavenging afresh. Her Stonehaven haul had vanished from their Land Rover. She suspected the technicians or the security detail when they had rearmed and supplied them. One sergeant had looked shifty. A grifter can always spot another. 'I worked my arse off for that money and jewellery,' she muttered. She'd vowed to keep it on her person now. A finger in the throw of rigor mortis snapped off. Imo whipped a diamond engagement ring into her pouch just as Jason was turning his head. She stood up swiftly, dropping the digit, pretending to watch their six, her weapon raised. Grinning, she knew the corpse had been loved. It was quite the stone.

Jason's eyes narrowed at her. Then he rolled them and turned back to the row of gazebos.

'Drop!' yelled Imo. She sighted her rifle and squeezed off a round. It barely missed Jason as he fell to the deck.

Looking ahead, he saw a middle-aged man in a leather waistcoat fall. His garment was shiny with blood that had mostly run off. 'Thanks. Bit close, though.'

'Naw, you had loads of time to hit the deck. I've heard you Air Force types are good at that.'

'Cheeky bitch,' he retorted, smiling. 'I guess you always played in the Army role in your Call of Duty gaming sessions.'

'Of course. Who plays RAF? When I played with the boys in the children's home, it was always Army. Nobody plays Navy either!'

Laughing, he replied, 'I'd never thought of that. I guess they don't.'

'Nobody ever plays RAF Regiment, dipshit,' interrupted the colonel. 'There are still four heat sources. Possibly five. The boffins think the last may have been a ghost signal. Now stop wisecracking and clear the area.'

Imo stuck her fist in the air, wrapping her fingers around her thumb to create a hole, pumping her fist up and down. Running to the fallen corpse, she checked it was dead, then entered the gazebo. An overwhelming smell of leather, like the aroma of a new top-of-the-range car, hit her, along with the comforting whiff of lanolin. She ignored the sheepskin rugs, the empty purses and wallets and headed to the back of the open tented area. Pulling down a black leather hat by its brim, she yelled, 'Over here, Cowboy.'

As Jason ran into the stall, he caught what she threw at him.

'It's not a magnificent Stetson like that dick, Bob, or Tex, or whatever his name was, but it'll suit you. C'mon Cowboy, get it worn.'

Beaming sheepishly, he plonked it on his head and leaned into the mirror on the adjacent tabletop. 'Cool, I like it.' Placing his rifle on the table, he whipped out his Glock, twirling it like a gunslinger in a Western movie. It fell to the grass, that was reddened in places. The colour from the stained pasture matched his cheeks.

'You dick!' she cajoled merrily. 'Keep the hat, Pippa will love it.'

Jason picked up his pistol and holstered it, leaning in for another peek in the mirror.

Spotting the petty cash, Imo lifted the lid quietly and slid out the higher value banknotes.

Tilting the mirror to the side in time to see her nimble fingers. 'Best get on. These trade stands are hiding four more infected. Or survivors.'

The next tent was full of tables. Upon them was an assortment of colourful beads, rocks, and crystals. 'People believe in this shite?' asked Imo as she scooped out a handful of pale blue and white gemlike pebbles and let them fall through her fingers like a stream of water.

'Whatever gets them through the day. I doubt they heal. The advertising slogans probably break many trade descriptions. But the positive thoughts they imbibe are beneficial.'

Imo threw one at him. 'Best you pocket one, then!'

Catching it, Jason held it up to the sun, mesmerised by its light and beauty. As he was turning it to make it glimmer, he was lifted off his feet. A head had powered into his chest, winding him. A rush of air causing him to groan as he fell, dropping his rifle.

An infected woman, wearing a flowing, flowery dress, ragged at the hem, was snarling, trying to bite him. A long, thick gloop of saliva fell from her open lips, revealing red, stained teeth. She released a gurgling noise as Jason wrapped his fingers around her throat.

The woman convulsed, as if orgasming as she was prone across him. Sabre stretched back, tail erect, legs splayed, teeth sunk into her left ankle, was yanking her backwards, growling deeply.

'Shoot her!' screamed Jason.

'I'll not risk shooting Sabre.' Imo walked casually to the nearest table, reading the label aloud, 'Chunky Rough Rose Quartz.' Scooping it up, she bounced it in her palm, weighing it. Then strode over to Jason, raised it to the sky and brought it down on the woman's head. A sound, like an axe hitting wood, resounded.

The snarling stopped, and the woman collapsed on Jason like a spent lover. Blood seeped from the embedded crystal. She rolled aside as Jason pushed her off with all his might. Screwing his nose at the fresh, acrid assault to his nostrils, he looked at her fatal wound, tilted his head, and vomited. Sabre ran round to give the steaming pile a tentative sniff.

Imo stuck out her hand and helped him to his feet. 'Heart Chakra my arse! Her positivity won't heal that wound! It won't attract much love, either!'

Colonel Winters clapped his hands, like a youngster at his first panto. 'Ha! We should make a video compilation of her quips. For the lads. For when they return from Ukraine. They won't believe me otherwise.'

The nearby senior technician's eyebrows lifted askance.

'Sergeant,' shouted the colonel. 'Arrange it, please.'

Shaking his head, no longer trying to correct the wrong use of his rank, the flight sergeant replied dutifully, 'Yes, sir. You leave it with me.' He scribbled away in his almost full notepad. The one for the Air Commodore.

Chapter 5

Walking more gingerly into the next trade stand, the plastic awning cracking like a sail caught in the wind, Jason tilted back his hat brim. He wasn't imagining things. The pile of chair throws and cushions had moved. A few muffled grunts escaped from the fabric and the figure moved towards the rear. 'Don't be afraid. You can come out now. We are the military. We are here to rescue you.'

The grunting, like the movement, ceased.

Imo entered the enclosed space, taking in the soft furnishing accessories. She'd never understood her sexes attraction to fluffy blankets and oversized and overpriced cushions. She lifted her weapon in disapproval.

Jason laid his palm flat in the air and pushed it down, up, then down again. He whispered, 'It's a frightened friendly. Poor thing thinks she's safe under that lot. In the dark. Like being a child under the bedcovers hiding from the Bogeyman.'

'Sexist. Could be a frightened bloke.'

He tilted his head. 'Fair dues. Lesson learned.' Nestling his rifle on a pile of white floor cushions the size of an adult's beanbag, he crouched and lifted the hem of the blanket pile.

'Come on out. I've a packet of peanuts here. You must be hungry. It's completely safe.'

Another groan came from the pile and the figure appeared to crawl towards the sound of Jason's comforting voice. It stopped a foot away from the hem of the uppermost blanket.

Jason reached forward and burrowed his hand under the pile, surprised at the weight as he scooped the fabric up and lifted them, creating a passage.

The figure broke free with a loud snort and a black snout burst out. Two setback eyes, partially covered by floppy ears, stared at him and a round face head butted him. A thickset black body, with a broad pink horizontal line like a learner swimmer's ring, sprang out and ran around the open-ended tent on all fours. Its short, twisting tail wobbling as its generous rump waddled. The British saddleback pig drew up short at a raised hackled Sabre. It gave a high-pitched squeal and darted off, making for the nearby trees and thick vegetation behind the tents.

Snot and spit blew out of Imo's face as she laughed. 'I thought we'd given up on saving pigs when we killed those police officers that arrested me!' She slapped her thigh with her free hand as she continued to snigger. 'I hope the eye in the sky captured that. Priceless! Your face. "Don't be afraid." I thought you were going to piss yourself.'

Jason stayed sitting by the blanket pile, heart racing. When he looked up at her, he smiled. He was watching the other heat source advance to her.

The infected man, dressed in black tailcoats, frilly shirt, and kilt, was swinging a wireless microphone like a stubby club at her head. He missed, and it bounced on her shoulder, black plastic breaking off.

'Ouch! What the actual fuck!' Turning, she saw the blood-stained stubble surrounding his puckered back lips and punched him hard in the jaw.

The Banchory Show Master of Ceremonies head snapped back with a growl. Crouching, he pulled a sgian dubh from his right thick white sock. With a sleight of hand, he yanked the blade from the scabbard and raised it back, ready to plunge it down at Imo's unprotected face.

A combat knife whizzed through the air and plunged into the attacker's throat. His sgian dubh dropped and blood-encrusted hands scrabbled at his throat as a torrent of blood cascaded down his frilly shirt. The lace failing to absorb the flow. The figure dropped to his knees, gurgling loudly.

Imo ignored him, turned to Jason. 'You could have killed me. I felt that whoosh past me.'

The flight sergeant grinned, double tapping his special badge with the crossed rifles. 'I never miss, remember?' He curtsied and pulled an imaginary skirt hem to each side. 'You're welcome!'

Hiding a smile, she kicked the dying man, so he fell onto his front. The grass softened the sound of his gurgling as he bled out. Imo picked up the fallen Highlander's knife, twisted it, appeared to weigh it in her hand and threw it over her shoulder. 'Cheap crap.' Pointing to the corpse, 'Want your knife back?'

Hand covering his mouth, taking deep breaths, Jason shook his head. Composing himself, he gulped and replied, 'I'll rearm when we return to the Landie. Let's move on and regroup there. I want to see what else is in the kit-bags.' He stepped around the pooling blood that was seeping into the earth. 'You think we will get through the fence? One day?'

Imo saw the look of yearning in his face, his creased forehead and narrowing eyes giving his emotions away. The jesting had been bravado, like she knew, deep down, she did herself. 'I always keep my promises.' Clucking to Sabre, 'I'll take the lead.' Giving Jason a wink, tapping her earpiece. 'Hey, numptee, how many feet away is the next heat source?'

'Call me by my first name, Poacher. We know each other so well now.'

She beamed at the use of her new nickname. 'Cool. Thanks. What is it?'

'Colonel!' Deep throated laughter echoed in their ears.

She stuck her arm out of the tent and raised her middle finger in the air.

'The drone operator is still detecting two more heat sources. Side by side, one fainter than the other. Five metres due east.'

Imogen whispered to Jason, 'What's that in feet and which way? The fucker didn't supply us with a compass.'

Jason brought his wrist up parallel to his chin and pointed. 'My watch has a compass.'

'Course it does, Cowboy. How have I lived without one of those for all these years?' She sidled over, eyes wide with greed.

Nudging her with his elbow, he warned, 'Don't even think about robbing it. Pippa gave it to me for Christmas.'

'She's got good taste. Can I have it when a zombie kills you?' she asked eagerly.

Slotting in a fresh magazine, he cocked his rifle. 'Not happening. Sixteen feet. Let's crack on.' He strode off, clucking for Sabre.

'That's my boy, both of you.' She grinned her toothy smile and followed, but not before flipping over the corpse, opening its sporran, and taking out a hip flask. 'Shame. I'm off the booze. But I reckon you owe Jason one for putting you out of your misery.' She admired the flask's decoration and pocketed it. Telling the dead man, 'My uncle would have loved that. He liked pheasants. Especially when he caught them for free from the local estates.' She ran out to keep up with her partner.

'This one's clear,' declared Jason, pointing to a trading pitch with enlarged photos pinned to vertical boards. There was a two-foot gap from the floor, and they were flush with the awning. The pictures depicted the Banchory Show from over the years.

At the next trade exhibition was a crisp white table-clothed stand bordering the edges of the open tent at waist-height. Decomposing floral tributes, like those left at untended gravesides, wilted around tightly bound tartan ribbon. A heady scent of pollen hung in the air. Imo flung aside the edges of the cloth, checking under the connecting tables. The Scottish Women's Rural Institutes members would have been offended by how she carelessly threw aside the flower and wreath displays. If any of the women had survived the onslaught after the chemical attack.

Seeing the stand was empty, Jason murmured, 'Should be the next gazebo, if your new best mate got his measurements correct.'

'He did,' came the god-like voice in their ears.

Two pairs of eyes rolled into the air. Imo slung her rifle, taking out her preferred close contact weapon. She slotted a heavy-duty ball bearing into her catapult, teeth bared back.

Jason followed, pivoting in a circle, checking their rear out of combat habit. He still didn't trust the colonel and his team of experts. Rifle raised to his shoulder; he took in the display stand of the St John Scotland organisation. They had been on a recruitment drive for Community First Responders in this rural area. Propped up on a clinical treatment couch was a woman, fresh blood seeping from open wounds to her two exposed breasts. She put her finger to her mouth, whispered, 'Shh,' and stated, 'He's finally got to sleep.'

Chapter 6

Imogen stowed her catapult, grabbed some dressings from the open first aid bag on the adjacent table and peeled them open. 'You'll be all right, love. You and your baby.' Spotting some disinfecting wipes, she tore these open, juggling the dressings and swabs like an experienced nurse. 'Let's get you cleaned up.' She dabbed away with the moist pads. Fresh blood trickled down the woman's breast as blood-encrusted scabs came away. 'Jason, keep a lookout for the infected that did this to her and find her a blanket or someone's shirt to wear. Sabre. Sit and guard.'

The black and tan dog, almost as tall as the couch, walked over and sat at the foot of the bench, looking out, as if affording the patient some privacy.

The woman rocked back and forth and from side to side, swaying her swaddled baby gently. She sang a lullaby that Imo recalled from listening to the carers from her children's home. Staff there provided temporary care for emergency admissions until they found foster parents. These were Imo's first encounters with the police, other than those who had taken her in after being hit repeatedly by her mother's latest boyfriend.

Retching a few metres away signalled that Jason was removing clothing from someone who no longer needed it. He returned, brushing down a chequered blouse and a puffer jacket. 'I thought she might be cold.'

'Thanks.' Turning back to the mother, still dabbing as gently as she could, Imo asked in a low voice, 'Who did this to you, love? How on earth have you both survived all this time, alone?'

The lullaby stopped. An eerie silence laid still in the tented enclosure. The woman tilted her head, looked from Imo to Jason, as if seeing them for the first time. 'Why, I'm protected.' Her hand dived into the top of the blanket, acting as a fluffy hoodie, and stroked her baby's head. The youngster's breathing sounded harsh from within the deep, downy material.

Jason and Imo exchanged a glance, and both shrugged.

'Who protects you?' asked Imo as she pointed to the wounds on the woman's breasts.

Jason gave them a quick, embarrassed look, then did a double-take and stared. He pointed. 'They are bite marks. Tiny. But bite marks all the same.'

Imo nodded. 'Could it be animals? Has the virus spread to them from humans, or could the air attack have affected them?'

They looked at Sabre.

Sensing their stares, the dog gave a low whine and a tentative brush of his tail against the grass.

'Good boy,' soothed Imo.

'That makes no sense. Animals would have attacked us by now if they had. Most have gone into hiding. Living off the land, returning to their base instincts.'

The lullaby restarted, sounding unnerving.

Imo put down the red-soiled swabs and gently pressed a dressing in place on one breast. The other was seeping blood around tiny puncture wounds, near to the nipple. 'Who protects you, love?'

Jason, amazed at how gently Imo was questioning and treating the woman, momentarily thought to his Pippa. He hoped she had access to kind and proficient maternity care. Would the National Health Service staff be overwhelmed? Jason doubted they had policies in place to deal with a zombie outbreak.

'Why, this little one, of course.' The mother beamed at her baby. 'The others don't come near us. They leave us alone. I take him with me when I go looking for food or need the toilet. This couch makes a comfortable bed.' She giggled. 'Though they can get noisy at night, the little devils.'

Jason's mouth flew open, and his eyes widened. 'You don't mean? No, please God, no, not that.'

The woman shook her head. 'Don't shout. Don't wake him up. My boy needs his sleep. He's been busy. My little angel kept me awake all night long. Feeding. He's such a hungry boy.'

More blood seeped from her wounds and Imo slapped a dressing on the other breast, being less gentle, not liking what she was hearing.

The blanket was shaking, and the baby started crying. This turned into a rough snuffling sound and then snarling.

Imo tore off the blanket, wrestling with the mother who was trying to snatch back her most treasured possession. Her blood loss got the better of her and she fell back in a faint. The blanket dropped, and the baby rolled against her right breast. It bared its gums, seeking its next feed with hungry, alert, red eyes.

Chapter 7

Jason and Imo took a step back, both whipping out their pistols, SA80's bouncing against their bodies, safe in their slings. Aiming their trembling Glocks at the snarling infant, but locking their eyes on each other.

'What the fuck do we do?' pleaded Imo, remembering the swimming pool in Stonehaven and her crimes against humanity.

'You do nothing, Imo. This is on me. The baby is posing no risk, and it's keeping his mother alive. Though with the amount of blood she has lost, we need to do something fast. We'll take her to Hazel, with her baby, and she can tend to her in the back of the cabin. We'll find them some transport and get them to bug out.'

Biting her lip, Imo nodded. Exhaling, she dropped her shoulders, tension surpassing. That's why he was the flight sergeant and had been forced to re-enlist. He could shoulder the big decisions.

'Kill it. Kill them both,' demanded the colonel into their earpieces.

Their jaws dropped and mirroring each other, they shook their heads, Jason's slow and Imo's fast.

'No way,' yelled Imo into her comms. 'It's a fucking baby, for Christ's sake.'

'That didn't stop you at Stonehaven when Flight Sergeant Harper's back was turned. Now kill it. And then the mother.'

Jason's head tilted.

Imo looked at the grass and muttered, 'I took no pleasure in that one. I didn't want you to do it. You are about to become a father. I didn't want you having terrible memories and guilty feelings.'

'Thank you,' croaked Jason, tears forming in his wet eyes. A droplet ran down his cheek as he looked to the infant, cushioned in the mother's lap, her hands loose around it. The baby continued to snarl and make biting motions.

'Obey me. Kill it. Kill the mother as well,' insisted the voice in their ears.

'No way, sir. I cannot comply with that order,' shrieked Jason as he paced around the couch. He raised his fist in the air. 'It's an illegal command.'

Sabre joined him, sniffing around a red patch on the grass.

Imo clicked her fingers and pointed to her feet, unable to form words.

Sabre obeyed and sat by her, staring up, sensing her distress. Nuzzling her legs, leaving slimy deposits on her combat trousers.

She tickled his ears and ran her fingers through his thick neck hair, relieving herself of some tension. 'What do we do?' she begged Jason, her voice cracking. 'It's an infant. The one I killed could move. It posed a threat. Maybe not to us because it moved so slowly. It was crawling. But it could have edged upon a sleeping victim.' She failed to convince herself.

Jason holstered his pistol, then took her free hand. Sabre whined. He missed the ruffling and ear tickling from his mistress. 'Leave this with me. You've heard me question my orders. You'll be my witness.' He waited for her to nod her head. 'The mother seems to be uninfected. I won't kill her.' He pointed to the canopy where the tentage was furled to create a doorway. He mimicked her rolling it down. Taking out his pistol, he mimed firing it into the grass.

Her eyes lit up with understanding, and her head was nodding vigorously. Winking, she walked away.

'Don't even think about it, hotshot. Obey your orders or you will be court martialled.'

A low-pitched whirring noise, like the quietest of lawnmowers, broke their numbed silence. Jason darted to the tent entrance in time to see a tiny drone take to the sky. 'They must be using several to watch our every move. Even the smallest are in operation. No doubt there are trackers on our equipment and on the Land Rover when they re-equipped us.

We must do as they tell us. I need Pippa and my baby to be safe.'

'That's right, Flight Sergeant,' mocked the colonel. 'You are my bitch. You'll obey my orders this time. No more Yemen incidents. Shoot when I tell you and at what I deem to be a legitimate target. Poacher, get yourself out of there. You don't need to witness this.'

'There has to be another way,' begged Jason, tears cascading.

'Remember, there is no cure. We don't know how long infections take to present after a bite. There will have been blood transfer. Kill them both. Think of it as protecting your wife and baby. You wouldn't want an infected to get over that fence.'

'Are they safe? Can I see them? I'll bring you survivors,' he implored his officer. 'Let me see Pippa.'

'Get on with it. That baby will grow and turn into a deadly infected. There is no cure, only more bloodshed, of the innocent. Obey your orders, Flight Sergeant.'

Bargaining, almost on his knees, Jason rasped, 'We can bring them alive for your scientists to examine. Tests might reveal why the adult infected have left baby and mother alone for all these weeks.'

'No one gets past my fence without my authority and certainly none of the infected. We cannot risk this getting out to the wider population. I expect to hear two shots within the minute.'

The flight sergeant in the control headquarters discreetly took out his notepad. He was patched into the comms via the communications specialist. Despite the comms and video recordings from the drones and CCTV being recorded, the flight sergeant still scribbled away. His eyebrows shot up when he next heard the answer his fellow flight sergeant got when he asked one last question.

Jason stood almost to attention, stretching his neck and raising his head defiantly. 'I demand to see your superior, please, sir. I'm assuming there is a brigadier in overall command of you.'

'No, there isn't. This is a wet job. Execute your orders, Flight Sergeant.'

'I want it on record that I have questioned your orders and requested to speak to your superior, sir.'

'Not noted, Harper. There is no law now. Only me. I've an armed drone above you. One hellfire missile will wipe out these infected and Imo, your handsome dog and you.'

'You'll never do it. You need us to carry out your dirty jobs. We are all you've got since your regiment deployed to Ukraine and neighbouring countries. Russia has kept you busy.'

Silence broke out across the comms, allowing Jason and Imo to exchange more shrugging.

A high-pitched whine shot through the air. The pair ran out of the tent. They felt the earth jump from under them as a missile exploded in the nearby corralled animal enclosures. Pieces of flesh, turfs of grass and earth sailed up in a dark cloud, along with the tattered clothing of the deceased. Hazel's truck rocked as slabs of meat and jagged metal from the fencing rained on the bonnet and roof. Muffled screaming escaped from the vehicle, but its doors remained tightly closed.

'That's a small taster. Now get it done. Colonel out.' The comms went dead.

Ashen-faced, Jason turned to Imo and whispered, 'I don't want you seeing this. Please take Sabre to the Land Rover. I'll return when my orders are followed through.' He stared at the grass.

Imo walked over to the woman, drawing out her combat knife. A hand restrained her.

'No, please. I must do this. You've done enough for me. I have my orders.'

Puckering her lips, she sheathed her knife and went to the woman's side. 'God bless you both. I hope there is an afterlife, and you are there together.' She placed her hand on the sleeping woman's hand. Imo immediately frowned. Then slid her fingers up to the woman's wrist. She paused for a few seconds. Turning to Jason as she walked out, she whispered, 'Maybe there is a God listening to us. You'll only need one bullet. She's gone, poor bitch. Her hand is stone cold. I can't feel a pulse.'

Tears fell freely from Jason. 'I'm glad she passed in peace with her beloved son in her lap.' He looked down at the baby nestled safely, a pair of dead arms lying on either side, as if saving him from falling off the couch. He slowly withdrew his weapon and bowed his head.

A low whistle from Imo caused Sabre to prick his ears up and follow his mistress as she went striding off. Crossing the arena, Imo heard a single shot echo around the King George V Park. The deep roar that followed would have woken this long-dead monarch.

Chapter 8

Jason ran across the arena, glistening eyes blurring his vision. Wiping away snot onto his combat jacket, feeling the rough texture of dried blood on his nose. He'd holstered his Glock, wanting to be rid of its reminder. His rifle banged against his back as he ran as if in self-flagellation. The pain didn't affect him. Running past the skatepark, he weaved amongst the dead. A gust of wind took off his leather hat. He didn't bother chasing it. Drawing up beside their vehicle, he leant against it, feeling the metallic heat in this August sunshine. He vomited and spat out, as if expunging himself of his sin. 'It's done,' he declared without looking at Imo or Sabre. Instead, he straightened up and leant in and took out a bottle of water, gulping deep draughts. With little left in the bottle, he offered it to Imo.

She shook her small bottle, green liquid sloshing within. 'Sorry, I was overdue my dose. I needed it.' Taking out her purloined hip flask with her other hand, she shook its contents. 'Drink this. You need it.' She carefully stowed away her methadone.

Without hesitation, he uncapped it, took a sniff, and drained its contents. His eyes watering more, springing wide.

Coughing, he handed the flask back and gave several coughs. In a husky voice, 'Whoever you pinched that from, he had good taste. A proper malt whisky. Thanks, I needed that.'

She whispered as she rubbed his shoulder, 'I'll get you a refill. Thank you for doing that. I don't think I'd have been able to.'

Turning to face her, he flung his arms around her and nuzzled into her neck, sobbing.

Still clasping the flask, she held her arms out impotently, thawed, and returned the embrace, holding him as tight as he held her. Remembering the woman and baby, she rocked him gently, making shushing noises as she stroked his hair. Part of her wanted to sing the lullaby, the other part knew it would be crass. She searched deep in her childhood memory for a comforting song or lullaby, but failed. Instead, she patted his back. 'This doesn't mean we are engaged or anything!'

He gave a brief laugh. 'Thanks. I needed that too.'

She pocketed the hip flask. 'Area secured. I guess Hazel can come out now?' She patted Sabre on the head, not wanting him to feel left out.

'No,' he answered adamantly, taking out his earpiece and tossing it into the back of the Land Rover. 'She's safe for the moment in her monster truck, fed and hydrated. I need to go somewhere. I'll drive. Take your comms off. We are on our own time now.' Jumping up the tailgate and into the cargo section, he unzipped the nearest kit-bag. 'First, I'd like to get some fresh magazines for my Glock and rifle. It's clear we must kill all the infected before I can get to Pippa. Let's rearm.'

She grinned. 'I've been looking forward to checking those out.' She watched him pull out a lumpy, dark green, cylindrical object, like a mini pineapple. It had a keyring type shape attached to it. 'What's that?'

Handing it to her, 'It's a grenade. From World War One or Two, by the looks of it. I thought the Government had shipped all the old ammunitions to Ukraine. They can't have run out already and are giving us the ancient stuff? It's called a Mills bomb. Pull the pin out, lob it and when it explodes, it fragments and takes out its surroundings. Just as efficient as our usual, modern ones.'

Imo juggled it between her hands, running her fingers through its pin, testing its tension. 'Cool, pass us a couple.'

She watched him open the long kit-bag wider. Her eyes lit up, then she scrambled inside it and pulled out a long, black rifle with what looked like a folding stock. Beneath the barrel was a pump action grip. Spotting the red cartridges with the gold rim, she stuffed them into her ammo pouch. 'Dibs the shotgun.'

'Know how to use it?'

'The clue is in the name!'

He furrowed his eyebrows and squinted his head at her.

'The poacher!' she exclaimed. 'I went hunting a lot with my uncle.'

'By hunting, we are still talking poaching, right?'

'Of course. Why pay for meat when it's just running around for free?'

'Okay. The L128A1 twelve-gauge Combat Shotgun.' He pointed with his finger. 'Telescopic buttstock, forend and round slot. Kills from forty to one-hundred and thirty metres. You might not want to extend the buttstock, though, given your size. Slot seven,' he scratched his head, 'Or is it eight cartridges into the tubular magazine? I only fired this once. Not in combat, just on the range.'

Talking over him, 'Yeah, yeah. Just point and shoot anything close by. Slot the cartridges in here and cock this back, then shoot the zombies.' She scanned the area eagerly. All she heard was panting and saw a lolloping tongue hanging out from Sabre. Shouldering her new toy, she used her teeth and free hand to uncap a water bottle. 'Sorry boy, hadn't realised you'd run out of water.' After refilling his bowl, she poured some over his snout to remove dried blood. 'That'll make you more comfortable.' She was missing the dog kisses and desperately needed one after what they'd all been through.

'You in the back with Sabre, or the front with me?'

'Ha!' She pumped fresh cartridges into her new toy. 'I'll ride shotgun!'

'Bollocks. I need their comms back. What the fuck are they up to?' yelled the colonel, his face reddening and veins straining fit to burst on his neck. He stormed out of the headquarters' main Portakabin. As he exited, the screen operators heard him screech, 'They don't get the better of me. I'll show them I'm in charge of this operation.'

Jason turned right out of the car park, Land Rover straining its gears and heavy load up the hill. The GPMG and its ammo, as well as the kit-bags, were adding extra weight. He took the left turn, into the main High Street of Banchory. It was eerily silent, save for the birds feasting on the decomposing bodies that were strewn across the pavements and road. The normally immaculate rows of artisan shops and cafes had their windows smashed in by looters. A body hung from one window; its head attached by a sliver of tendons. A dried blood pool decorated the pavement below its overhanging throat like a disgruntled employee had thrown paint. A knitted doll tableau topper above the town's main post box displayed a pirate scene straight from a children's book. The jolly pirate with the eyepatch looked as if he approved of the violent outbreak that had occurred.

Pointing, Jason remarked, 'The windows of the cafes and shops are the ones that have been put in. They've left the opticians alone. It's a sign of looters. There must be survivors hiding out somewhere. Perhaps in a housing estate or the nearby school. That's what I'd do. We haven't seen a vehicle that is road worthy yet. Most have had their tyres deflated or punctured. I haven't had time yet to examine them. Something is going on here.'

Imo kept her head poking out of the open window, shotgun extended. She was hoping for her first kill, not blackened corpses. They looked ghastly, with their shrunken gums and protracted teeth, like they were grinning at her misfortune. An overpowering smell of rubber hit her as they passed the hardware shop, and she crinkled her nose. Turning away, she spotted the local pet shop with the suitable name of Stinky Beasties. She made a mental note to go exploring for something to spray on Sabre. He really stunk.

Jason swung the vehicle to the left and parked at The Stag Hotel. The three storied building had an almost Mock Tudor look to it with its black painted lintels and window frames. Its sterile white exterior was in sharp contrast to the pools of red that surrounded the corpses spread around the welcoming benches and seats.

'Cool. I can fill up my pheasant hip flask. What do you fancy?'

'Maybe later,' replied Jason, pointing to his right. 'That's where I want to go. It felt disrespectful parking outside there.'

Looking over, Imo exclaimed, 'The undertakers! I think we've had enough of dead bodies. I guess the funeral director is also dead, otherwise he'd have had his tape measure out and cleared this mess.' She kicked the nearest body. Then wiped her boot on its skirt. The corpse's guts had spilled out like a bundle of rotten sausages. A noxious smell pervaded the area. 'Why would you want to visit there? Nice old stone building, though, looks like it had a bell in the small tower.' She made a ringing noise and shouted, 'Bring out your dead! Bring out your dead!'

'Not there. Though I wish we could have put that poor mother and baby somewhere respectful, like in one of the resting rooms.' He was silent for a few seconds. Jason pointed to an obelisk with four pillars and a spire with the four compass points. Rows of names were carved on the four sides of the granite. He walked over the road, twisting between the abandoned cars, ignoring the bodies that were beyond their help. Reaching the plinth, he knelt by a large poppy wreath. Bowing, he recited the Lord's prayer.

Walking behind him, Imo recognised that the monument he was kneeling by was the war memorial. The only charity tin she wouldn't steal from pubs and shops was the Poppy Appeal. Even she had standards. She heard his voice falter at 'Forgive us our sins.' He broke down crying, hands spread across the names of the brave Gordon Highlanders who had died during the Great War. She continued the words, stretching far back in her mind. Keeping her eyes open, she reached, 'Amen,' and remained silent.

Jason ran his hands up and down the long list of names, repeating, 'Forgive me,' as his fingers dug deep into the stone. Rising to his feet, he walked around all four stone facings of the high obelisk, repeating his mantra, tears flowing freely. With each side he beseeched, 'It was a baby!' His wails echoing, disturbing the feeding birds.

Imo scanned the area, keeping Jason safe.

A black suited man ran from the stone building behind them, his shirt was stained red. A green plastic apron flowing from his neck, like a superhero cape, in the wind. Its ties were flapping uselessly in the air.

Imo grinned and brought her shotgun to her waist, shook her head, then dug the stock into her shoulder and took careful aim. In her peripheral vision, she could see Jason continuing to feel the names on the war memorial. His tears cascading, shouting, 'Just a baby!' Crouching, she carefully placed her new toy on the ground, knelt and withdrew her catapult.

The man was almost upon her, and quick as a flash; she let off an aimless ball bearing. It whizzed through the air, shattering the man's shin bone. He stumbled and fell to his face and crawled towards her, grinding his teeth.

Imo put away her catapult and withdrew her combat knife, a present from the colonel's team. The harsh rasp of metal on its sheath caused her to grin with delight. She ran to the man, jumped in the air, and brought it down into his skull, twisting as the blade drove through bone. Coils of grey matter spurted out from his head and then blood pumped out, covering the brain matter. The man dropped to the ground, his back hunched as arms and one leg supported him for a few seconds. He then flopped over as Imo withdrew her knife and wiped it on his suit. 'Never did like undertakers. Greedy fuckers. The amount you charged my aunt when we buried my uncle. Creepy-fingered fucker.' She gave him a kick, wishing it was the Aberdeen funeral director who had ripped off the only relative she had left. She gave his corpse another kick. 'That's for trying to overcharge me when I buried my aunt a few months later.' Squatting, she brought her mouth to the corpse's ear. 'Not that I paid the bill to the creep who owned the undertakers in Aberdeen.' Looking up proudly, she glanced across to the war memorial and shouted, 'I ran off with the life insurance money and had a holiday!'

Her boast fell on deaf ears. Jason was gone.

Chapter 9

Whistling sharply to Sabre, while scooping up her shotgun, Imo glanced across to their Land Rover. It was empty. 'Where's the stupid fucker got to? He'll get himself killed, without me.'

Sabre's head squinted to the side; his ears cocked.

She smiled at the dog's actions. 'Of course! Go find, boy! Find Jason.'

Giving an excited bark at this new game, a black snout dived to the pavement, gave a quick lick of the fresh blood and brains, and sniffed in circles. His tail was half erect, hovering in the air, making tentative movements left and right. Then excited circular movements, and he bounded off, crossing towards a tree and shaded grass area. His snout was working furiously on the ground, and he took Imo to a small church, set well back from the main road. A sign boasted it was the St. Ternan's Scottish Episcopal Church.

Running to its slate-roofed porch, Imo took the steps in one bound and pushed the heavy wooden doors. They wouldn't budge. She ran around the stone building and tried to see through the tall, narrow stained-glass windows, but the trees obstructed most of the light. 'Find Jason,' she repeated.

Sabre's nose was twitching as he traced the scent of his master around the grassed area and circled around picnic tables and chairs from the church café. He leapt onto the High Street pavement and ran, nose to the floor, to the next building, a taller, modern structure.

'Another church!' exclaimed Imo, spying the ugly gargoyle that jutted from the side of the stonework. Looking further up, she spotted another directional sign. This one had a cockerel. There was also a tower, complete with clock facings. She recalled the converted church building she'd shot at earlier in the day. 'I guess farmers were religious in their day. And needed to know the wind direction and time.' In an ironic voice, she told Sabre, 'Bit of overkill, though, three in one street.' Glancing at the sign that gave the service times, she noted the name, saying it out loud, 'The West Church. Is this where our boy is?'

Sabre sat in front of two glass doors with a long metal handle on each. His tail was brushing the flagstone floor.

Trying the right door, her eyebrows shot up in delight, and she made her way into the dark interior. Taking the circular staircase, she curved her way up its tight passage, Sabre leading the way.

His tail had stopped turning like a helicopter's blade, and he was sniffing furiously. Giving out a sudden yelp, he tumbled down the stairs as a body sprang on him. They toppled, coming to a halt when a liver-spotted, wrinkly hand got caught in the bannisters. Snarling teeth matched the ferocity of Sabre's and a deep growl came from the recovered dog as he bit hard and through the other hand. The woman in the dark blue dress with white spots tried to stand, but Sabre continued to bite and tug at her arm, blood spraying on the walls. Her other hand snapped like a twig, and she flopped backwards, her head banging onto the metal banister, splitting open.

Imo sprang, grabbing her long, flowing hair into a ball, yanking her head back, exposing her neck, slitting it from end to end. Ignoring the gurgling noise, she kicked the dying woman down the stairs and tussled Sabre's neck with a blood-stained hand. 'You okay, boy?'

Sabre barked once, bounding off, Imo hot on his heels, shotgun at the ready. Reaching the top step together, they entered a large balcony with rows of old-fashioned pews. The heady smell of ancient wood overpowered Sabre's nostrils, distracting him from Jason's scent. He sniffed the air a few times and didn't see the man with the matted, curly black hair and home knitted jumper run towards them, roaring. He clutched a bible in one hand, as if warding off the devil. In another, he carried an ornate gold cross on a wooden plinth.

It was about two feet high, and he used this to make swiping motions at Imo.

Raising her shotgun to her shoulder, she tucked the stock in, muttered, 'Forgive me, Father, for I have sinned,' and fired. The blast echoed around the church and hit the man full on the chest, shooting him backwards as the recoil forced Imo onto her back. As she fell onto Sabre, she saw the man fly over the front pew and over the guardrail. She glimpsed an altar in the background below and heard the man's body crumple as Sabre gave out a sharp whine of protest. 'Amen!'

Dusting herself down, she reached over and ran her fingers over Sabre's fur. 'Thanks for the soft landing, mate. Just as well I'm a lightweight.'

Sabre gave another head tilt, eyes not leaving his mistress.

Walking down to the front pew, Imo peered over the balcony. There was a small stage where the altar lay and behind it was an organ whose brass pipes proudly rose to varying heights, the tallest to the ceiling. On either side were more modern musical instruments, including a drum set. In front of the stage was a low wooden lectern, lying on its side, its head protruding from the two steps onto the red-carpeted stage. In the central part of the area were rows of much more comfortable chairs with built-in red cushioned backs and seats. The once neat rows were askance but sitting on the one nearest the altar was Jason, deep in prayer, arms folded together, body leaning forward. Behind him was a woman in a dark suit with one sleeve torn off, shoeless with ripped hosiery, inching towards him, arms outstretched. Imo could hear her snarling.

Chapter 10

Quickly realising that she would not survive a jump down from such a great height, Imo ran, retracing her steps back down the flight of stairs.

Sabre dashed in front of her, his bum wiggling with each twist and turn. His paws jumped on the elderly woman Imo had shot, causing fresh blood to pump out. Her corpse expunged a groan of escaping air as he scampered over her.

Imo gave an involuntary shiver at this deadly groan, winked at the corpse, and bounded down the stairs.

Dog and owner reached the glass doors together. Paws were scrabbling uselessly at the thick glass. Imo took hold of the handle and pushed. Someone had locked them. She reached into her pocket, drew out a dog biscuit, and threw it up the stairs. 'Go find!' she ordered Sabre as she drew her shotgun to her shoulder, leaned in for the recoil, and shot the door.

Glass shattered backwards, sprinkling the red carpet with shards that looked like thick ice. Imo used the stock of her shotgun to clear a passage. Glancing down, she ordered a returning Sabre, 'Sit and stay. I'll put your special boots on when I finally unpack those kit-bags. That fucker of a colonel had better have supplied them.'

Jumping through the gap, Imo ran to her right and into the main church hall.

Jason was deeply engrossed in prayer, moving back and forth while uttering words swiftly, as if a spirit possessed him.

The woman in the shredded suit reached him. A blackened set of hands were wrapping around his throat.

Jason continued his rocking, dragging his opponent back and forth, like they were making the beast with two backs. His prayers came out as screeches, then choking, as he struggled for breath.

Her grip tightened, and she leant forwards, teeth bared, mouth wide open as if about to take a bite from an apple. As her drooling lips reached Jason's neck, a black shotgun stock crashed down on her skull. Dazed, the woman released her deadly grip as a booted foot kicked her away from her victim.

Imo smirked as she raised the shotgun, pumping a fresh cartridge in one smooth action. 'Prepare to meet your maker, God botherer.'

The shotgun blast took the woman full in the face and neck, snapping her backwards. Her body toppling the chairs next to Jason, and she sprawled, legs in the air, exposing her satin red underwear.

'Filthy bitch!' laughed Imo. 'Someone dressed for church this morning.' Pleased with her joke, she turned to Jason, expecting a wise crack in return, or at least a laugh. Instead, she saw him rocking in his chair. Then he sprang forward onto his knees, hands clasped, like he was begging. His eyes were on the empty altar, where the cross should have been.

Sensing movement from the other side of the congregational seating, Imo spied another middle-aged man in a jumper, edging towards her. His skin was blackening. In contrast, his mouth was encrusted with blood. 'Someone needs to give you guys fashion tips. You'll never get laid wearing jumpers from the eighties.' She laid her shotgun on the nearest seat and withdrew her catapult. Seizing a large ball bearing, she loaded and twanged her elastic in one deft movement.

The deadly metal ball crushed through his nose; cartilage flew in the air as the fatal missile buried deep. Blood flowed like the heaviest nosebleed. The man dropped onto his back and gave a few dying gurgles as blood pooled in his throat.

The large drum on the stage rolled across, bouncing down the steps. 'Thank you!' exclaimed Imo. 'I've never had a drumroll before.' She bowed as the cymbals gave out a crash as a figure emerged.

Imo squinted her eyes, unsure if this was a friend or foe. Pulling out one of the Mills bombs, she felt for its pin and wrapped a finger around the thin metal ring. She smiled as she saw the red eyes leering back at her. Pulling the pin, she lobbed the grenade overarm, like a cricketer. The spoon lever flew off, pushing down the bomb's hammer pin with a sharp crack, like a Christmas cracker. Its fuse was now lit. She immediately jumped onto Jason, pulling him down to the floor. She shielded him from the blast with her thin body, chest protecting his face, like a nursing mother.

Wood, bits of carpet and red flesh rained down on them. A shard of bone embedded itself into the back of Imo's combat webbing, burying into the canvas, stopping short of her jacket.

Through her ringing ears, Imo could hear Sabre barking. 'Wait,' she yelled, her voice sounding muffled. Rising, she tried to bring Jason to his feet.

He resisted, curling into a ball instead. In this near foetal position, he recited the Lord's Prayer. His hand was near his mouth, almost sucking his thumb.

Scanning the room as she rose, Imo stood over Jason. She drew back her hand and slapped him hard, reddening his cheek.

'What the fuck!' he exclaimed, rising to his feet, reaching instinctively for his pistol.

Nodding to his weapon, 'Glad you are back with us.'

Jason turned to the altar. 'What have you done?'

The thick altar table lay splintered and askew. Its purple tablecloth was in tatters. The lectern was embedded in the remains of the man's torso, his legs ragged. Hanging from one part of a torn drum section was a shredded arm, its finger pointing at Imo, as if in accusation.

'Just doing the Lord's work!' she drawled, aiming for a Californian accent, and failing.

'Fuck!' exclaimed Jason, looking around. 'You've destroyed the altar. It's sacred. You've not even left the cross.'

Grinning, she nodded at the Pastor, who had fallen from the balcony. The cross was sticking proudly through his chest, where he had impaled himself as he fell, releasing his grip on the heavy, gold-gilded object of worship.

Jason belched. 'I'm not even going to ask. And Sabre?'

The dog had ceased his barking when he heard human voices. 'Sitting patiently by the door. We had a blast at the decorated window. The door scene of the gathering of the harvest with the salmon and sheep might take some putting back together.'

Grabbing his rifle, he quickly checked his magazine. 'That's someone else's problem. I've made peace with my God and fellow man. I've got my orders to follow through. Let's get out of here and leave these poor souls at peace.' He strode out, crunching underfoot like virgin ice protesting at being disturbed.

Imo followed obediently, beaming, relishing her kills. She knelt by the corpse of the woman and yanked off a chain with a gold cross, gathering it up and stowing it with her other booty. 'Lord bless you for your donation.'

Chapter 11

Sabre ran between the couple as they inserted the earpieces of their comms. His tail swished and curled around their legs until a sharp screech broke through their earpieces. Two human heads tilted, and teeth clenched at the noise.

'Where the fuck have you two been? I want active comms at all times.'

Imo glanced at the hotel, squinting her eyes to see through to the bar. 'Fuck off, Colonel. My boys need a drink.' Pulling out her hip flask, she made for The Stag Hotel.

'We'll see about that,' retorted a smug voice.

The familiar buzzing filled the air and from the clouds erupted several drones, their blades whirring furiously. They flew in front of Imo, blocking her way.

Waving her arms around, she tried to swot them away, but they simply rose and fell back in line. 'The fuck they going to do, give me a little sting, like a bee?' She felt a tapping on her shoulder.

'Behind you,' whispered Jason, like a lame pantomime dame.

Imogen gulped as she turned. Hovering down the High Street was a grey miniature-like aeroplane. The cockpit looked like someone had painted it over in a dull grey. Its wingtips spread across the road and pavement, almost touching each row of shops. Behind its front wheels was a black and yellow-ringed row of missiles.

'Best do as the Colonel says, Imo,' sighed Jason. 'He's mad enough to fire those hellfire missiles at us. We'd never survive.'

Laughter filled their comms. 'That's right, best you two get onboard with the mission. Remember your written orders before you went off script? I left them on your Land Rover's driver's seat. One of our cameras saw you open the envelope. You've secured the area. Now I want your targets alive and at the border by the end of the day.' As if to reinforce his words, the MQ-1, the Predator drone, advanced towards them, rose and flew over them. Sounding like a vacuum cleaner on overdrive, its front camera swivelling like a wandering eye. Its wingtips lights flashing like it was winking mischievously at the trio below.

Sabre was barking furiously, his hackles raised on a ridge, the fur pointing upwards from his back, like a punk had gelled them.

'Enough!' shouted Jason. 'We get it. You are in charge. We'll do as we are ordered.' Returning to the Land Rover, he filled his pouches with grenades and rifle magazines.

Imo reluctantly returned to their vehicle and armed herself with more shotgun cartridges. Rummaging in a bag of military clothing, she pulled out four leather and canvas stump looking boots. Whistling for Sabre, she gave him a dog treat to chew on while she strapped his new footwear on, ensuring the Velcro fastening was tight enough.

Gulping it down, the dog mouthing at the Velcro fastening until he spotted another dog treat sailing through the air.

'You'll soon get used to your canine boots.' Pointing to her own military boots, 'They'll feel like a second skin.' She threw more treats to take his mind off them.

The Land Rover screeched to a halt outside a building that looked like someone had dumped a Swiss chalet onto the edge of a car park. The dark brown wood reached high to an apex roof. Below this was the trefoil, the three-leaf clover sign of the Girl Guides with a star within the uppermost leaf. The grills on the window by the ramped entrance reminded Imo of her prison days. The area was eerily silent. 'You sure there are heat sources, Colonel?' She shivered at the memory of those almighty missiles.

'About twenty of them. In the back hall. Gain entry through the door on your right.'

'Yeah, tried that. It's bolted from the inside.' She hammered on the door. After waiting with an ear to it, she hammered some more. 'Nobody's home.'

'Gain entry. Use the explosives.'

Imo snapped around and glared at Jason. 'Have you been hiding the goodies again?'

He winked. 'Guilty, as charged.'

Rummaging under the front seat of their vehicle, he pulled out a dull brown block with yellow printing that looked like a bar of gold had lost its shine. He also held grey wire, almost like thin rope, slender and yellow, like an electric cable, and a roll of gaffer tape. Whistling as he strode to the door, he attached the block to the middle of the doorframe, where he judged the bolt to be on the other side. Coiling the slim grey rope along the doorframe, taping it down as he went. Then he trailed a thin coil of yellow wire down the ramp. He held this and uncoiled as he went around the building. 'Best fall in behind me and keep a hold of Sabre.'

Watching the dog and his pal stand behind him, Jason counted from five. As he reached two, Imogen grabbed the wire, shouted, 'Fire in the hole!' and tugged the wire.

A detonation echoed around the building as chunks of wood flew in the air and erupted in front of their vehicle. One lump banged against the side of their Land Rover, making a dent in the metalwork. Several large fragments rained down on the sloping roof of the building and slid down and perched in the guttering, like man-made icicles. 'I guess we are in,' declared Jason, shouldering his rifle.

'Brilliant!' yelled Imo, releasing her hold on Sabre's collar.

'Got any more of that stuff?'

Jason rolled his eyes. 'Look beneath the ammo boxes for the GPMG, I hid some there. Don't go crazy,' he warned. Looking at the glint in her eye, he knew he was wasting his breath. He joined her as he ran up the ramp. She had her shotgun at the ready.

'Forget the first rooms. There are no heat sources there,' ordered the colonel. 'Go to the main hall.'

Jason walked behind Imo. She was leaning into her weapon, eager fingers on the trigger and the pump action. He took the time to check the rooms. Before he could go into one, it opened a fraction. A pair of wide eyes and an open mouth peered around the door. 'Are you the police? The army? I've seen what it is like out there. I had to protect my girls.'

'You are okay now. We are here to guide you to safety. You did the right thing, bolting the door. You stopped them from getting in.'

The door narrowed as she shut it, but not before he saw her eyes widen even more. 'You don't understand. I didn't bolt it to protect them. I bolted it to protect others from them.'

Chapter 12

The door slammed. Jason cocked his head at Imo and nodded towards the hall. Reaching the fire doors together and bending low, they peered through the thick glass panel at chest height. The inside was smeared with blood. They squinted through each pane of glass on their side of the doors. Young girls in ripped red clothing were wandering around in a daze. Their shredded clothing revealing how black their decaying limbs had become. Each of their mouths were caked in dried blood. Three near-naked adults laid sprawled across the middle of the gym-like floor, like human caterpillars. They were covered in bite marks. Red footprints led away from them.

'Christ,' muttered Imo. 'They are infected. All of them.'

Jason gulped. 'Now we know what happens if they don't get fresh blood, their cells degenerate. Look at the colour of their skin. They are like walking corpses. The poor souls.'

Imo thumped him on the shoulder. 'Don't start that again. I don't need you ruminating.'

They both jumped up in alarm as a soft voice behind them explained. 'They attacked the other leaders and helpers. Some were the mothers, helping us out. I only escaped by pushing them away. They had such strength, though, for little ones. As I battled away my attackers, the other adults turned the same way, and all hell broke loose. I pushed, kicked, and punched my way from the hall and somehow locked the doors. I've tried to go in since, but keep getting attacked.' She rolled up her sleeves to reveal deep scratches. 'It's the same if I go outside. I've been living off the store cupboard supplies since. Drinking cold hot chocolate powder is disgusting, especially as the water supply seems to have been turned off.' She turned away. 'I had to take the toilet cistern lids off and scoop out that water.'

'You did the right thing. We'll leave your girls here and get you to safety.' Jason was about to ask her how she survived the chemical attack, but his comms came to life.

'Forget that!' barked the colonel to Imo and Jason. 'Get in there and kill them. Then you can play the saviour with the pretty Guide leader.'

The armed couple gulped. Jason turned to the Guide leader. 'What's your name?'

'Raven.'

'No, I mean your Christian name. Not your Guiding name.'

The woman scowled and, through gritted teeth, replied, 'That is my proper name.'

'Ah, sorry,' Jason's face reddened.

A round face thudded into the left door's glass pane, its teeth snapping uselessly as it slid down.

Raven shrieked. 'That's Amelia. What on earth am I going to tell her mother?'

Imo pumped a fresh cartridge into her shotgun. 'That's the least of your worries. Give me the keys.'

Raven stared at their guns, shook her head, and screamed, 'No. You'll kill them,' as she bolted through the passageway and ran outside.

'For fuck's sake, why do I always get the runners?' sighed Imo as she held her shotgun aloft and gave chase.

'Bring this one back alive this time. It'll be easier with the key.'

Sabre's tail swished through the doorway, barking at what he thought was a fun game.

The Guide leader stumbled on the debris outside and swerved to her right, sprinting down a path that ran along the side of the hut. It led to another path with tall shrubbery on each side. Brushing past the foliage, she pumped her arms like pistons to gain speed.

Imo, hot on the heels of Sabre, let out a breathless expletive at the speed of the woman.

Raven ploughed on through the toddler's amusement arcade, running past the small motorbikes on their single circuit. Young bodies were sprawled over the handlebars and several of their mums and dads laid prone on the mock circuit, as if protesting at an oil refinery or major motorway. The only glue attaching themselves to the ground was deep pools of long-dried blood.

Giving a gasp at this gruesome sight, Raven dived through a gap in the low white picket fence that led to the fairground's mini waltzers. These giant teacups would normally gently rotate its inhabitants around. Instead, the bodies were slumped in their seats, with heads toppled forwards.

Imo, fed up with running, laid her shotgun on the nearest picnic bench and drew out her catapult. She rummaged in her pocket for the smallest ball bearing. This would nip the skin and perhaps stop the woman. Cursing, she could only find the large, lethal ones. Jason's words rang in her ear, guiltily. Killing the infected was one thing, but not a survivor. She didn't deserve that. Imo stuffed her slingshot back into her pocket, grabbed her shotgun, and sprinted across the road. Panting, she wished the ice-cream shop on the corner didn't smell so bad.

Gasping hard, Raven swivelled her head around, looking for somewhere to hide that didn't already house corpses. She looked in vain at the dull pink harling on the maisonette style flats separated by an entrance to a self-contained car park. Peering in the shop window of a beauty salon, she gave a gasp at the corpse that was spinning around in a hairdresser's chair. Its head was tilted back, like it was having its hair washed or an open razor shave. Its throat looked like a blunt, straight blade had repeatedly sliced through it. A blackening woman in skinny jeans and a close-fitting top was absently pushing the armrests of the chair each time it halted. Raven left them to this macabre waltzer game, having learned weeks ago not to disturb the infected if she wanted to live.

Spying the disused Aberdeenshire council offices, she tried the door and cursed when she found it locked. Looking behind her, she saw the near emaciated figure in military uniform, wielding a shotgun, gaining on her.

Raven bounded up the concrete stairs, ignoring the street artist decorated walls. She tripped and banged into the glass side of the local library. The side of her face that had smashed into the tall, wide windows glanced at the children's books. Her Rainbow pack would have appreciated these gentle, fun stories. Snorting, then crying, her eyesight blurred, then was off focus with tears. She drew her knees to her chest, sat, and rocked.

Sabre drew up alongside her, barking excitedly at this catch me if you can game. He cocked his head as his new friend screamed at him, rose, and ran off. Looking back at a panting Imo, he ran to her, circled around her once and bounced off, sniffing around the ramp. Spying a hole in the wall, he gave a few sniffs at the empty drinking fountain that had been salvaged from the long defunct Banchory Railway Station on the old Deeside Line.

'Stop fucking around, Sabre,' gasped Imo, almost doubled over. 'Go catch her,' she pointed to the woman who was trying the doors of a pancake café.

Yapping excitedly, Sabre bounded along the twisting ramp, following the scent of the woman.

Imo jumped up the stairs, two at a time, reaching the Scott Skinner Square before her canine companion. Following Raven into the café, rank with the sweet smell of decomposing food mingled with the acrid, sharp hit of dried blood, Imo wrinkled her nose. She raised her shotgun to her shoulder.

Raven mistook Imo's grimace for anger at her running off and screamed, 'No! Don't shoot me!'

Imo pulled the trigger and as the blast hit an apron wearing woman full in the chest, she pumped another cartridge and blasted her weapon again. A thin lady, high bouffant hair matted with blood flew back as the shot took her full on the face and neck, blasting off her head. The old-fashioned hairdo cushioned the fall as the skull and what flesh remained landed by Raven's feet like a punctured basketball. The traumatised Guide leader let off a blood-curdling scream and ran to the door.

Imo hit her full in the face with her padded combat gloved knuckles.

Raven dropped to the floor, dazed.

'Keep still if you want to live. Stay in here. I'm not chasing after you again, you stupid fucker. You could have got us both killed.'

'I wouldn't have cared about me,' sobbed Raven, rubbing her nose. She checked her hand and arched her eyebrows at finding no blood.

'I was talking about Sabre and me. I don't give a flying flock about you.' Imo stretched out her palm.

Raven, mistaking her action, thrust out her hand for a help up.

Imo swotted it away with the shotgun's barrel and placed one boot on her chest, pressing down, hard. 'You really are a stupid fucker. The keys. Give me the fucking key to the main hall. We've a turkey shoot to get through.'

Raven shook her head, 'No, you can't. They are so young. There must be another way.'

Imo pumped a fresh cartridge and pressed the barrel end onto Raven's forehead. 'I can't be arsed going into all this again.' Sighing, she looked at the pleading eyes below. 'There is no cure. Their parents will be long dead. Look around you. It's lucky you survived. Did you have a mask on when the Russians attacked?'

Raven shuddered as she spied the bloated stomachs and purple-blackened skin of the four corpses under the nearest table. Four middle-aged women out for their sweet treat, coffee, and gossip. This would have given them lots to talk about. She nodded. 'I was worried about the new strain of Covid. The youngsters pick it up and spread it so easily at Primary School.' Looking around and shaking her head, she sighed, 'That was the least of my concern. There doesn't seem to be any point in wearing a mask now. I wondered what happened. It was some sort of invasion?'

Imo yawned. 'It was a chemical attack restricted to Aberdeen and the Shire. It turns people into brain-dead killers, blah, blah.' Pushing down on her weapon, she snarled, 'Just give me the key. Jason isn't here to stop me having fun.' With her free hand, she unsheathed her knife, the sharp rasp of the metal on metal disturbing the menacing silence.

A wet patch formed around Raven's navy trousers, seeping onto the carpet of the café.

'Don't fret, they all do that,' jibed Imo, remembering the shop assistant at her last armed robbery. 'That key better not be in your trouser pocket.'

Red-faced, Raven retrieved the key and held it out. It glistened with moisture in the light.

Imo nodded to the counter. 'Find a towel over there and clean it, then bring it back.' Hearing a low rumble from behind the doors that led to the bathrooms, Imo hissed. 'Keep well back, but stay in here with Sabre.' Turning to Sabre, she planted a smile, revealing her stumpy teeth. 'Guard, boy.'

Booting in the door, Imo let off a joyous string of expletives as she pumped her shotgun and blasted away.

Jumping at each blast and subsequent heavy thud, Raven rubbed furiously at the key, then slid the towel between her legs and wiped. She threw it towards the sink, not caring that it fell to the floor. The café was a charnel house and more mess on the floor would not matter.

Imo returned, pocketing some sealed chocolate bars before grasping the key.

'You aren't military, are you?' Raven challenged, hands on hips.

'He is. I'm along for the ride. Let's get going. Stay a few steps behind me. Don't try running off. I won't chase you, but the zombies might.'

She stuttered, 'Zombies!'

'Yeah, that's what I call them. Killers would be another word for them. The infected is what my partner calls them.' Laughing, she watched Raven look nervously around.

'You are going to kill them all, aren't you?'

Imo replaced her smile with pursed lips. In a low voice, 'I'm sorry. There is no cure. I'll make sure it is quick and painless for each of them.' Slotting some fresh cartridges into her shotgun, she beckoned to the door and whistled for Sabre. 'Let's go. Time to get some youngsters to the Rainbow Bridge.'

Chapter 13

Ashen-faced, Jason took the key from Imo. 'We need to be fast. I've watched them through the glass. It's like they are in the playground, skipping around, playing tag. They return to the bodies and rip chunks out of them, chewing as they run around. That's why they've lasted so long. They are vicious.' His body shook.

Imo furrowed her brows at Raven. 'We'll need you to open the door, then get out of the way. Can you do that?'

Raven shook her head, sobbing. 'I won't be a part of this. I can't watch.' She wiped her nose on her navy top.

'She's right,' declared Jason. 'We forget. These last few weeks have almost dehumanised us.' He gently took her hand. 'Follow me. There is a woman called Hazel, hiding in one of those monster trucks, where the Banchory Show was held. It'll be comfortable enough in her cabin, they are roomy. I'll see you safely there.' Nodding to Imo's shotgun that was leaning on the door, 'Perhaps the SA80 would be a better option for what we must do?'

'I'll come with you and check what's in the back of the Land Rover. Want me to drive you both there?'

Shaking his head, 'The walk will do me good. I need a caffeine hit, maybe bring me an energy drink.'

'How can you talk of drinks at a time like this?' moaned Raven.

'We've been through a lot and done some unpleasant things. I'm afraid it's becoming the norm for us. We must refuel.'

Raven whistled low. 'Your poor souls.'

'Yes,' was all Jason could bring himself to say as he led her out of the building.

Pulling aside debris from the earlier explosion, Imo jumped up to the back of the Land Rover, rummaged around, and passed Raven two cans. Reaching in her pocket, she pulled out two chocolate bars. 'Take them, the shops are always open, for us!' Turning away, she delved into another kit-bag and whooped in delight. 'What a beauty. I'm having this!' A thick cylindrical object, about twelve inches in height, tapering at the bottom was thrust into her deep pocket, lower down her thigh. A thin loop of brown, fraying rope-like cord dangled from her pocket. She jumped down, ignoring her SA80 rifle.

The colonel paced the Ops Room, muttering about 'picnics' and 'walks in the park.' His operators kept their eyes glued to their screens. Clicks on keyboards broke the silence between his oaths. He squinted over to his second-in-command as the Flight Sergeant slid a notebook into his breast pocket.

Jason stood in front of the monster truck and waved his hands in the air, shouting, 'Hazel!'

A face peered through the windscreen in a gap not covered by the thick, slimy trail of blood and animal guts. Half the face of a goat lay in the centre of the bonnet, what looked like liver was squished into the front fenders.

'It's safe to open up.' Jason wedged the ladder into the grass, leaning the top rung against the vehicle, allowing space for the door to open.

Hazel opened the passenger side a fraction. 'Are you sure? Who's that with you? Is she one of them? What was that almighty explosion?'

'Calm down,' replied Jason as softly as he could. 'She's not infected. I need her out of the way and somewhere safe with someone who I trust. Can you look after her, please?'

The door opened further. 'What about me? Will someone rescue me soon? Can they take me away from here?'

'Soon. Yes. I'll find you some transport. All the vehicles around here seem to have several flat tyres.'

'That's the activists. We had to chase some of them away from our trucks. They jammed lentils into the tyre valves. To deflate them. Most drivers only carry one spare, so they deflate at least two tyres.'

Biting his lip and recalling the crashed cars they'd seen throughout the town, Jason replied, 'They've made life complicated for us. But don't worry, we'll find you a vehicle to take you to the Aberdeenshire and Angus border.' He ushered Raven up the ladder. 'Now close the door and only open it for me. I'll be back soon.'

Turning, while lowering the ladder, it surprised Jason to see Imo sat on the grass, staring back towards the Guide hut. She was cuddling Sabre. Every few seconds, she ran her hands through his fur. The dog shuffled forward on his bum and brought his muzzle to rest on her left shoulder. Jason could see her shoulders shudder and her back shake. He waited a few minutes to let her tears subside. Reaching into his pocket, he quietly opened a bag of nuts and devoured them.

Sabre's ears pricked up at the rustle and he raised his snout to sniff the air. Then he gently lowered his chin and allowed his mistress to continue her tight embrace.

Coughing as he approached, Jason saw her release her grip and wipe at her eyes. 'Imo, let me do this. I've made peace with God. I've got my orders to carry out. You stay here with

Sabre. For me, it's like the brave service people of both World Wars who had to kill their fellow man to stop a greater evil.'

'No,' she whispered. 'We are a team. I'm your partner. We'll do this together.' Rising to her feet, she slotted cartridges into her shotgun.

Jason banged a fresh magazine into his rifle. He hadn't the heart to ask her to use hers instead of the shotgun. Rapid fire might be quicker. He grasped her hand and was surprised to feel her grip back. 'Let's make sure we are quick and there are no survivors. I don't want them to suffer any more than they already are. This chemical attack was a bastard. Those Russians are inhumane.'

Nodding, Imo led the way, clucking for Sabre.

Wrinkling her nose, Raven passed Hazel a can of energy drink. 'Been hiding long?'

Red-faced, Hazel replied, 'Sorry about the smell. I've been in here since the chemical attack, using a bucket as a toilet. I tried going to one of the Portaloos from the show, but those infected people would attack me. How I fought them off and got back to the safety of the cabin, I just don't know. Every time I snuck out at night to forage for food amongst the catering trucks, I would empty my potty. It's left a lingering smell because I can't rinse it out.'

'They have turned the water supply off. I've had to go into the same toilet without flushing. Sorry if I smell. I haven't been able to shower.'

Hazel burst out laughing. 'We are a right pair. Are there many survivors?'

Crying, Raven shook her head. 'My Rainbows are dead or infected. Those people in the military uniforms are off to kill them. There is no cure.'

Reaching over, wide-eyed, Hazel cuddled her. 'You mean they are off to shoot them?'

Raven simply nodded. 'And there is nothing we can do.'

At the fire doors to the main Guide Hall, Imo stared at Jason. 'I won't go early. I'm taking this one seriously. You count down and I'll turn the key, thrust open the doors and duck out of the way.' She had left Sabre at the corridor's entrance, guarding their back.

'Just to be clear,' replied Jason, cocking his head. 'I'll take care of those furthest away. You cover my front and shoot any that slip past.'

Nodding once, she raised her grenade. 'I'll throw to my left before blasting away.'

'Pitch as far back as you can. We don't want any shrapnel flying at us. These Mills bombs were designed for trench warfare. The earth sides would have shielded the blast from the throwers while decimating the enemy.'

Making the sign of the cross, grenade and pin jiggling like rosary beads, Imo shrugged. 'Hedging my bets. This must be my worst sin.'

Jason counted down.

Imo shoved the key in the lock, turned it and thrust open the doors. She pushed hard against the stiffened wood. Blood had gummed them together. Rolling to the left, unpinning her first grenade, stopping at a crouch. Throwing it overarm, it landed by two children feeding on a corpse. Ignoring them, Imo immediately tugged free another grenade and lobbed it further. It came to rest by a squatting child, thick drool slavering down to the wooden floor. It was staring straight at them as she urinated.

Jason, unable to release the grenade overarm in the limited space, threw it underarm as far as he could. Sprinting into the hall, he drew the pin from another grenade and launched this one further. Dropping to the floor, drawing his rifle, and shouldering it as his belt buckle hit the deck. Spurting out three bursts of fire at every moving target.

Imo had no time to shoulder her shotgun as the first explosion tore into bodies. Metal chunks from the 'pineapple' grenades digging deep into virginal flesh.

On the second explosion, limbs were thrown into the air like a macabre juggling act. Lumps of flesh fought with splinters of bone to reach the apex roof. A tentacle-like piece of bowel wrapped itself around the flagpole, its flag crimson and dripping.

The third explosion tore through wooden tables, its splinters acting like darts. They pierced a child, imbedding deep, leaving tiny tips like acupuncture needles. These didn't heal or bring peace. Nor did they take away pain. They just brought instant death as blood poured out from multiple holes.

The last explosion, a second later, detonated mid-air, releasing its metal fragments at high velocity. This rapid, molten-hot shrapnel ripped through several thin necks. Its velocity mincing the young skin, dicing through muscle, ligaments, and bone. It sheared off one head, and it bounced in the middle of the hall. The rampaging survivors kicked it about like a team game as they snarled and roared their way to the two intruders.

Imo cradled her shotgun, estimating the distance to be about forty metres. Shooting, she took no pleasure in seeing a child with bouncing ponytails shredded. Her ragged uniform dyed bright red from the immediate blood loss. Imo gulped and sought another target, whispered, 'Forgive me,' and fired. Another four-foot-high figure sprung backwards as if on elastic.

Jason quickly wiped his eyes, needing to focus through his tears. He continued to fire and ensure he'd sent a fatal shot.

The screams from the survivors and dying mingled, built to a grisly crescendo, and then faded away as the hall was thick with white smoke and the smell of cordite. A small fire broke out from a hewn table that held paperwork. A pair of white trainers with red blotches laid on the edges of the flames. Its occupant was still, its trousers and underwear torn clean off in the blast, revealing stark white limbs with mottled black patches.

Jason wanted to run towards her with a blanket and cover up her modesty. Instead, he slid in a fresh magazine and continued to fire.

One girl broke through the smoke and was within feet of Imo. The shotgun disturbed her snarl in mid-bite as it blasted a hole through her chest. The short-range cartridge tore clean through her and embedded itself into the open mouth of her school friend. They landed together, almost hand in hand, as if about to go off skipping. The child behind them slid in the spurting blood pooling on the floor and came to a halt by Imo.

Dropping her shotgun, unable to take a clean shot without harming Jason, Imo screamed in anger at what she had to do. Withdrawing her hunting knife, plunging it deep into the youngster's chest, almost pining her to the floor. She immediately withdrew it with a sickening, squelching sound. Plunging it back in several times, Imo waited until the kid's hands were no longer scratching at her throat.

Jason squatted, one hand in a pool of blood, the other holding his weapon. Gasping, he leaned forward, was violently sick, then stood up, leaned into his rifle, and fired at a girl, head down, running, and roaring. Her skull blew apart, face unrecognisable as a human. Her legs buckled, and she dropped to the floor, neck gushing blood in the gruesome red swimming pool that had once been a hall of fun.

Hearing footsteps behind them, Imo ducked in time as a tyre lever was thrust at her head.

'STOP THIS!' bellowed Hazel, looking into the hall with wide eyes.

Twisting around, shotgun raised, Imo glimpsed Raven in the corridor, petting Sabre with tentative strokes of a shaking hand. 'No treats for you tonight, boy.'

Sabre whined, then nudged Raven's hand with his muzzle for more strokes.

'You two are inhuman,' continued Hazel. 'You can't get away with this. They are children.'

'You fucking what!' exclaimed Imo, the bloodlust rising in her, pumping a fresh cartridge into her shotgun.

Jason turned around to face his accuser. He struck out his hand to block Imo's aim with her shotgun. 'Stay out of this Hazel, you don't understand. We must -'

His legs buckled, and he dropped to his knees as a child ran into him. It made growling noises, then leapt at Raven, sinking its teeth deep into her neck.

Sabre sprang at the child, dragging it off his new friend, shaking the youngster's ankles.

The child lost its grip, ripping a lump of flesh from Raven's neck as Sabre dragged her off the Guide Leader, teeth gnashing.

Raven gave a drowning gurgle as blood flooded her throat. Still on her back, she spurted a fountain of bright red blood, coughing once, before spasming and lying still.

Jason whipped out his Glock, aimed, recognised the child as Amelia, and shot her through her forehead.

Turning with a glare, Jason growled to Hazel, 'You see what you have caused? This is on you. She was uninfected, saved others from her Rainbow pack, and is now dead.' He raised a rigid finger and pointed at her chest. 'You did that. To an innocent woman who only did good in her brief life.'

Hazel dropped her metal weapon. 'I didn't realise.' Her voice lowered. 'I didn't think they'd be so vicious.'

'Why?' sneered Jason. 'Because they were children.' A shotgun blast caused him to spin around, weapon raised in defence.

'That's them all,' declared Imo, her voice cracking. 'I'll just walk around, make sure they are dead. I don't want the little ones suffering any longer.'

'Thank you, Imo,' he replied in as gentle a voice as he could. After she'd walked a few paces, he deepened his voice. 'Hazel, come and see what these innocent children did to the other Guide Leaders and helpers.' Jason twisted around with a grimace plastered on his face, ready to pull Hazel around the hall. To shove her face down into the faces of the dead. Into Raven's face. The woman was gone.

Chapter 14

Using her combat knife, Imo prised off the ends of two shotgun cartridges. She tipped the gunpowder out into a straight line, going as near to the fire doors as possible. Throwing down the empty cartridges, she grasped bundles of paper from the surviving notice boards hanging on the wall. As she walked along to the start of the gunpowder trail, she kicked wooden debris until it formed a makeshift bonfire. Stuffing sheafs of paper into any gap, she also gathered any torn clothing and heaped this upon the wooden bundle. Running back to the other end of the gritty black powder, she took out a zippo lighter, gifted from an earlier corpse, and lit the gunpowder. It sparked, ignited, and trailed along the floor in a bright orange line, throwing up random black ash as it went.

Imo sprinted for the fire doors, glancing at the large camping stove gas cylinders stored in a line against one wall. She pushed them onto their sides, rolling them to her bonfire, not waiting to check they reached her intended target. Instead, she pelted down the corridor, grabbing her weapon on the way out. Reaching the fresh air, she doubled over and vomited. Spitting out the last of her regurgitated most recent meal, she retched one more time.

Jason approached her, took hold of her shotgun, and rubbed her back, like she was a friend leaning over a toilet bowl in a nightclub. He looked on with a frown. His friend was wan, eyes sunken, her cheeks hollow.

'I can't do this anymore, Jason. What have we just done?' Remembering the gas cylinders, she demanded, 'Take me away from here. Now. I need somewhere peaceful. Just a nice meal. I know it's ready rations. But maybe we can eat them in a beautiful place, away from all the dead.'

Taking her hand, Jason led her to the Land Rover, opened the door and helped her into her seat. He laid the shotgun in her lap and noticed she did not grip it.

Whistling for Sabre, he scanned the area and spied a black and brown furball sprint from the other end of the park. Jason waited until the dog had jumped into the back. Grabbing its collar, he rubbed his face into the dog's thick neck of fur. 'Extra hugs for your mum when we stop. I know just the right place.' Securing the tailgate, he jumped into the driver's seat, spun the car around, and as he was turning left, an almighty explosion ripped through the Guide hut. The wood from the chalet-like sides fractured and hurtled through the air in all directions. The roof disintegrated and collapsed, allowing thick flumes of black smoke to gush out.

'They deserved a cremation. We can't bury them, and it didn't seem the right thing to do to just leave them in that state, rotting away,' sobbed Imo.

Jason reached over with his left hand and placed it on hers. He remained in first gear, driving slowly away, like a laden hearse leaving an undertaker.

The colonel shouted down the microphone, his words falling on deaf ears. Jason and Imo had removed their earpieces, his words coming out as an indistinguishable low-level screech in the back of the Land Rover. 'Track them,' he ordered the first of the small drone operators. Tapping the shoulder of the nearest video operator, he ordered, 'Patch into the roads CCTV and any buildings that have them. Get them on screen. NOW!' he yelled.

Swerving between the crashed cars, Jason glanced to his right. The plush green lawn of the bowling club was scattered with white trousered men. Their once white shirts were crimson patched. Several skirt-wearing women had their dignity snatched away from them in death and Jason looked away from their raised hems. As he glimpsed the large lawn roller with the red handle, his eyes were drawn to the tennis courts set further back. A body was weighing down the net. It appeared to sway in the wind. The tension from the net fighting against nature.

Looking in his side mirror, he saw the proud blue metal supporting arches of the bowling green pavilion. The shattered window of their tearoom had a blackened arm wedged in the glass. It dangled onto the blue window frame, as if trying to escape the horrors within. There was another flagpole. This one was clinically white, unlike the horrifying Guide hut one. This outside pole reached high and allowed its flag to flutter peacefully in the passing breeze.

The sloping fence, designed to keep vandals out, had a body embedded in it, like a soldier caught in barbed wire in no-man's-land. His hand was reaching out too, seeking help.

Looking discretely across to Imo, his heart sank as he saw her head was down, tears freely flowing, shoulders shaking. He grasped her hand tighter.

She looked up, pointed to her right, and a smile broke through momentarily. 'Thank, fuck. That must mean they are alive.'

Jason drew up alongside a totem pole carved from a red cedar tree. Atop was a magnificent eagle, painted blue and white. Its wings were spread majestically. A yellow beak bore down on them. Below it were carvings honouring an exchange trip to Ontario, Canada, in happier times. There was the Scout sign, a Canadian leaf emblem, a green and purple thistle, and a black and white killer whale.

Beyond it, taped to the windows, filling them, were 'Help' signs, painted in large letters on paper taped together, like a morbid arts and crafts afternoon had been held in a church hall. Above the windows, a large professionally made sign declared the building to be the 1st Banchory Scouts.

Jason took his hand from Imo's and handled the gears. 'Let's leave them for a few minutes. They've waited this long. Kept alive all these weeks. I need to take care of you first.'

Biting her lip, forcing back the tears, Imo muttered, 'Thank you.' Fresh tears fell.

Leaving her to cry herself dry, Jason sped away down the tree filled road, following its twists and turns. Taking a left turn, he came to a halt before a narrow bridge, chocked full of crashed cars. 'Sorry, we are on foot here for a few minutes.' He gulped as he looked through the mesh fencing of the bridge. 'Wait here.'

She stayed still, save for the shudder of her shoulders as she cried.

Jason gently closed his door, released Sabre, and grabbed their rucksack with their brew kit and rations. Shouldering it, he held aloft his rifle at the ready.

Seeing her furry friend paw at her door, Imo dried her eyes, opened her door, and tried to jump down.

Two paws leapt onto her, and a dry tongue washed away her tears.

Giggling, she snorted, 'That tickles!'

Jason rooted into his pocket and passed her a packet of dried beef. 'Feed him as you cross the bridge. The poor lad's hungry.'

Sabre jumped down and sniffed as Jason gave the packet to his mistress.

Imo walked away, cradling her shotgun, juggling the packet and passed a treat every few seconds. Sabre swallowed them whole, not even stopping to chew. A brief smile passed over Imo's quivering lips.

Jason sighed, his shoulders dropping in relief. He didn't want her looking to their right. The river gushed a torrent of red water, and corpses were crashing against the rocks. The violent swell crushed faces against the mighty boulders. Limbs were tangled and wrenched free. A baby, face unrecognisable, smashed from rock to rock as if it were on a ghastly see-saw. Jason leant forward and dry-heaved. Wiping his mouth, he joined his friends across the bridge and pointed to a cottage to their left. 'The tearoom has a charming garden. I'll light our stove and get a brew on. I can't give you sandwiches and scones, but I bet our rations have something tasty.'

'Yeah, that fucker of a colonel doesn't skimp on the food. I'll give him that.'

Jason smirked. Glad to have the old Imo back. Pointing beyond the gravel car park, he led her through a small wooden fence and into a sloping garden. The plush grass led down to the River Dee, and he steered her away from there. The overhanging tree branches, which looked lush in green, concealed the sight of the river. Remaining above, he placed his rifle on a wooden table, wiggled the rucksack off onto one side of the seat, and pointed to the opposite. 'Get yourself comfy and give Sabre the rest of the food. Then I reckon he's earned a chance to chase the nearby squirrels.'

She giggled like a teenager on a date. 'My uncle and I loved to shoot squirrels. They are quite tasty. Sabre will love them. Go play, boy! But only catch the grey ones.' Imo watched as the dog went scampering off.

Lighting their stove on the tabletop, Jason dug out a small pot, filled it from his water bottle and set it on the top. Using a small penknife blade from his pocket, he sliced through the brown tape, securing a ration box. 'This looks like a ration pack from the eighties. Do you think the military is running low on these, too?' He didn't wait for a reply. 'I hope they checked the expiry date. I bet we find a packet of Spangles in them.'

'Spangles, are they some sort of special underwear?'

Jason roared with laughter, upsetting several wood pigeons from the nearby tall trees. They flew off in a huff. 'No. They were a square sweet with a dimple in the middle. The best ones were fruit flavoured. Great to suck on apparently and keep you awake on guard duty. Not really my generation. He pulled out a tube. I'm more the dextrose tablet generation. The old sweats, those close to retirement and long served, used to love reminiscing about Spangles.'

'I'd rather have a pot noodle.'

Nodding to the trees. 'Watch the birds, they are relaxing. I love their cooing sound and fluttering wings. That totem pole eagle looked fun.'

She grinned. 'Thank you. I just need to recharge, you know?'

'I know.' He patted her hand as the water spluttered. 'Coffee?'

'Yes, please, followed by a caffeine drink chaser. Then those Scouts won't know what'll hit them!' she jibed.

'I've patched into the Falls of Feugh restaurant CCTV, sir,' declared the screen operator. She used her mouse to zoom in on Jason and Imo.

'They are having a picnic. All they need is a tartan rug and a chintz tablecloth. How decadent. I wish we could communicate with them. I'd give them a piece of my mind.' The colonel tightened his grip on his coffee mug, fingers going white.

'They are allowed to eat and drink, Colonel,' added the flight sergeant absently as he buttoned his breast pocket.

Plonking his coffee mug down on the nearest table, spilling the black fluid, causing the nearby technician to swipe away his paperwork, the colonel strode over to his second-in-command. Leaning down, he thrust his face into the flight sergeant's. 'When I want your opinion, I shall ask for it.'

The flight sergeant rose, meeting his officer's gaze as the colonel rose. The two men remained eyeball to eyeball. 'That team deserves a break. They need to eat and drink. I wouldn't ask my squad to perform as well as Flight Sergeant Harper and Miss Pritchard are doing, without nourishment.' Pausing, he added with a curl of his lip, 'Sir.'

Left eyelid twitching, the colonel looked down to the breast pocket of the man in front of him. His hand rose, then swiftly dropped. 'Yes, well. You may have a point, Sergeant.'

'Flight, or Flight Sergeant,' corrected his junior, loud enough for his team to hear.

'Noted,' replied the colonel, walking back to the screen. His eyes narrowed, and he turned to an adjacent technician. 'Make the small drone do a fly past. Drop it as close to their picnic as possible. Fly it around their heads. Let them know we are watching.'

'Sir,' acknowledged the drone operator.

Imo smacked her lips. 'Love a bit of corned beef hash. These boil in a bag meals are so easy. I don't know why you military types are always whinging about your diet.'

Jason grunted. 'Try living off them day by day.' He slapped his forehead with his palm. 'Just like we've been doing these last few weeks. They play havoc with your bowel habits.'

'Missing your daily paper and sit down to read every morning, are you?' she ribbed. 'Thanks, I needed that coffee and a meal. What's for pudding?'

A low droning noise disturbed the local bird population. It broke into the gentle rustle of leaves and the flow of nearby water. A whirring object grew larger as it descended from the sky, buzzing around them like a swarm of bees detecting nectar.

'Someone is pissed with us,' laughed Imo, sticking her middle finger in the air.

Turning his back to the drone, Jason passed Imo a light green pouch. Steam rising from its open contents. 'Chocolate pudding in a rich chocolate sauce.'

Licking her lips, Imo's eyes lit up. 'I passed an ice-cream shop earlier. My sweet tooth wanted one.'

Laughing loud, for the drone microphone, 'Your one remaining one!'

Imo smiled at him, revealing her stumpy, black teeth, 'Fuck off, Cowboy!'

Jason grinned. Mission accomplished, he thought, relieved to have his friend back. He crinkled his nose at the remaining dessert. Who eats ginger pudding in a rich ginger sauce? He thought as he reluctantly picked up his spoon, looking for Sabre to share it with.

Chapter 15

Striding back to their Land Rover, comms back in their ears, ignoring the outbursts from their colonel, Jason tapped Imo on her shoulder. 'Best not look in the river.'

'Are you kidding! I love that river. That mesh fencing on the bridge didn't stop me scrabbling down as a youngster. It's the season, you know?'

Jason cocked his head.

'For the salmon to leap upstream.'

'Ah,' his eyes lighting up. 'The Poacher!'

She beamed. 'I would sneak out from the children's home. This was in the days before my aunt and uncle got custody of me. My uncle and I would stretch a net across first thing in the morning. Before the tourists and their cameras came to watch the fish leaping. We'd sell them to his usual contacts. Best pay day ever!' she boasted. 'Premium fish. Tasty too. My aunt would have the barbecue all lit up for our return and we'd season one, wrap it in foil, along with some giant potatoes. What a meal!' Her eyes had a faraway look in them as she was momentarily lost in the past.

'That's a lovely memory to have. Don't spoil it by looking.'

'Don't worry. I'm back to my old self.' She spun to her left, watching a near naked body hit headfirst into a jagged granite rock. Plumes of rushing white water gushing over him, washing away the lower red torrent. 'Blimey, that would make a rotten paddleboard.' She watched as several more bodies crashed into the huge rocks, the sound of the crunching of their bones lost above the din from the cascading, churning water.

A lone salmon, a sheen on its multi-grey flesh, leapt from the water and flopped back into the torrent. It was swept away like it was going from mashing machine to washing machine. Spinning in the deep red chaos.

Above, in sharp contrast, was a canopy of green from the overhanging branches. The salmon were seeking their old spawning grounds, hoping to bring new life into this dystopian horror.

Wanting to take his mind from the ghastly sight below, Jason shared a memory with Imo. 'I'm glad we didn't go into the restaurant. I've a happy memory of sharing an afternoon tea with Pippa there. I loved how light the rooms were. We always got the table by their window, next to the stone fire that reminded me of a wishing well. It was electric, but looked like a log pile was aflame. It was homely, and they stuffed the tiers on the afternoon tea with mini cakes and generously stuffed sandwiches with their crusts cut off. The chefs would make their own scones, and we'd tease each other about putting the jam or cream on first. I always drove there so Pippa could have a glass of prosecco. A great treat whenever we travelled through Deeside.' Nodding upstream, 'I doubt there are many survivors in Aboyne, Ballater and Braemar.'

Pursing her lips, 'I guess we might find out after we've cleared this area and rescued any survivors. I hope the Royal Family is safe. I think the King and Queen will be in residence at Balmoral Castle. They may not have escaped the yellow fumes.'

'I never took you as a royalist.'

'My aunt loved all that. Some of it rubbed off. Though I wouldn't spare my catapult if a certain prince came wandering past.'

Grinning, he suggested, 'Let's leave this place to our memories and rescue those behind the help signs.'

Pumping a cartridge into her shotgun, she yelled above the cascading flow of water, 'Time to go scouting for boys!'

An axe was thrust out of the first-floor apex window above the porch. 'We are armed. Are you infected?' a bedraggled, uniform-wearing man shouted.

'We are here to take you to safety. Can you come down and open the door, please?' shouted Jason.

'Who are you?'

Imo raised her black shotgun and ran her hands from her head to her feet, over her combat uniform. 'The military, you daft -'

Jason interrupted her. 'We'll take you to safety,' he repeated.

The window was slammed shut.

Imo scanned the notice board, reading and wondering if the building contained Beavers, Cubs, Scouts, or the older Explorers. Laughing, she tapped the noticeboard with the shotgun's muzzle. 'They are having a laugh. The Banchory Moosehunter Explorers! What a dipshit name. I bet they'd crap their pants if they came face-to-face with an almighty moose and its giant antlers.'

Sabre barked and ran around her, wanting to be part of the game. He followed his mistress as she walked up the ramp and joined Jason under the porch roof.

A bearded face, jowled cheeks and sagging eyelids stared through the window. His eyes looked bloodshot, but uninfected. His sweat-stained, light brown shirt looked equally tired. It could have done with a spin in the Falls of

Feugh natural washing machine, thought Imo as she nodded at him.

Despite his ragged appearance, he wore his yellow and blue Scout scarf in a neat roll. It was tied securely near his throat with a leather woggle bearing the Scout emblem. He raised his right hand to shoulder height, thrust three fingers in the air and made a loop with his thumb and little finger.

'Dib, dib, dib,' shouted Imo, gleefully.

Jason acknowledged the greeting with a brisk military salute to his forehead, four fingers splayed.

The door opened, and a head popped out, looking from side to side. 'Thanks, I now know you are of sound mind.'

'Ha! I wouldn't be too sure of that!' chortled Imo, leaning her shotgun over her shoulder.

The Scout Leader looked from one to the other and spotted Jason's rank insignia. He squinted at Imo's uniform. 'Oh, you are the RAF. And you are?'

'With him,' sighed Imo. 'Going to invite us in?'

'Sorry. Yes.' Opening the door wider, he explained, 'I don't know what's been going on. We've lost all signals from our mobiles and each time we try to leave the hut, we get attacked by violent men and women. I've kept my boys and girls in for their own safety. Is it some sort of virus?'

Imo barged past him, and Sabre rushed through his legs. The Scout Leader splayed them to allow the dog to pass without damaging his sensitive parts. Over her shoulder, she parted with, 'You explain. It's your turn.'

Jason rolled his eyes, took the Scout Leader by the shoulder, turning him around. 'Did you have all your mouths and noses covered a few weeks ago?'

Scratching his head, the Scout Leader shrugged his shoulders. 'An odd question.'

'Odd times,' replied Jason absently. He scanned the corridor, noting the stairs to the left and patrol rooms to the right. They built most Scout huts on the same principles. Though, this more modern one had two floors. He knew the main hall was a few steps in front of them. 'There has been an enemy attack. The chemical distributed by a plane infected people. Made them attack others.'

'You are kidding!'

Rolling his eyes again, Jason retorted, holding up a bloodied hand, 'Do I look like I am kidding?'

'Sorry. It sounds so unbelievable. But then who would have thought Russia would invade Ukraine? My troop's generation should not see war. Our ancestors fought to prevent such things.'

Shrugging, 'I'm still fighting for them.'

The Scout Leader shuddered as he looked down at Jason's bloodied uniform. 'Sorry. You said you are here to take us to safety. Where is that?'

'Further south. Near Dundee. The military has erected a fence around Aberdeenshire to keep the infected in. Along the A90 is an entrance. Head for there. We'll find you transport, somehow.'

The Scout Leader returned to the door and squinted out through the glass. 'Where's the rest of you? Is there a truck for my troop?'

'It's just us. No further soldiers can be spared.'

'Oh. I'm Dave, by the way.' Thrusting out his left hand, he quickly withdrew it when he remembered how bloody Jason's hand was.

'Jason. She's Imo and our dog is Sabre.'

'Mufflers!' exclaimed Dave. 'We had an open campfire at the back of the hall, in the garden, to demonstrate making twists, a kind of doughy, sugary treat on a stick that is cooked over logs. It gets smoky, so we cover our mouths with our Scout scarfs. Would that have stopped the fumes infecting us?'

'Seems so. You are all lucky. You survived the Russian attack.'

Dave looked at his brogues. 'Not all of us. Simon, my assistant, didn't have his scarf around his mouth. That's when he turned feral. Beastly, really. Like a rabid dog. The boys and girls thought he was putting it on until he attacked Lucy, our other assistant leader.' He looked away. 'Killed her outright. Ripped her throat out there and then. That's why I believe you when you say the Russian's weapon makes people attack each other. That's when I picked up the axe and buried it in his head. Instinct. Will I go to prison?' His eyes were watery.

'That's above my paygrade, I'm afraid. I doubt there are even laws to prosecute under for these types of situations.' He couldn't help but wonder what crimes Imo and he were guilty of. He knew the colonel was probably recording through the drones and patched in CCTV.

The Scout Leader paced around the corridor, rubbing his hands. 'I did my duty by protecting the boys and girls. I locked all the doors and windows and ignored the bangs against the wood and glass. We erected the signs. Every day and during the night, I tried to leave, to get help, but there were always people trying to attack me.'

Jason, wanting to take the Scout Leader's mind off the distressing incidence asked, 'How did you manage for food and drink?'

'Camp stores. Our policy is always to restock the dry goods straight after our summer or winter camps. The jerry cans were already filled with water. Not enough to shave or wash in. I had to limit them to drinking only. We could heat the water up and cook with our gas stoves. We are about to run out, though. Our camps are usually only ten days long. I've stretched the meals out, what with my two leaders not needing to eat.' His voice trailed off.

'You've done well. I need you to gather your Scouts and tell them what has happened. Prepare them for what they'll face on the journey. There will be lots of dead bodies, most decomposing. Arm them with any more axes you have, or other weapons. I doubt any are firearms trained?'

'I am.' Dave tapped a cloth badge with a circular target below the Scout's emblem on his arm. 'Well, just the air pistol and air rifle, strictly speaking.' Waving his axe, 'I also qualified in tomahawk throwing. It's a Master at Arms activity badge,' he boasted, standing up taller.

Imo wandered in from the hall, a teenage boy following her. 'Cowboy here has one, too. Mine is in the post.'

Jason handed his pistol over and watched as the Scout Leader checked the magazine and reloaded the weapon. He nodded in approval. 'Good. Anyone with red eyes is fair game. Shoot to kill.'

The youngster made a chopping action. 'Cool, that's what happened to Simon before he ripped Lucy's throat out. You should have seen Skip here. He sprang into action and buried his axe in his brains.'

'Who's your new pal?' asked Jason.

'Can't shake the fucker off,' moaned Imo. 'Loves my shotgun.'

The Scout pointed to his leader's hand. 'Cool, Skip. That's a Glock 19. Can I have a turn?'

'No, Austin. Please go back to the hall. Gather up the others. I'll come and join you and tell you all how we are to be rescued.'

'Skip?' asked Imo, ushering the boy away from her.

'I like to use the old-fashioned titles. It's short for Skipper. It creates a sense of discipline and respect.'

'You'll need it. They must keep safe out there and do what they are told by you. Break it to them gently, but their families probably haven't survived this.'

A tear fell from Dave's face. 'I have a wife and daughter at home.' Wiping it away, he lifted the pistol. 'Is there no cure?'

Imo and Jason shook their heads.

'How will we get away to safety if there are just the two of you and your Land Rover? Will you make several trips?'

'No. We have orders to evacuate civilians, but to keep in the area, to clear this sector. I'm afraid all the local cars have crashed, and most roads are blocked. Imo and I had to drive across farms and fields to get here. We can't even take the farmer's trucks from the Banchory Show.'

'My Scouts and I were due to give a demonstration there. That's why we gathered here. One last rehearsal. Aren't there lots of trucks?'

'I'm afraid the activists have rendered them useless.'

'Not lentils again? Don't they realise farmers need these types of vehicles during the winter months?'

'Yes, that's exactly what has happened.' Jason pursed his lips. 'I'm not sure how you'll get away. It doesn't sound far, but not on foot. You'll be prey to every infected for miles.'

Imo grinned, causing Dave to take a double-take when he saw her open mouth for the first time. 'Don't worry, I have an idea!'

Jason groaned. 'Not another train,' he moaned as he recalled the Stonehaven Land Train. Then grinned.

Beaming, Imo boasted, 'They should be faster than that and can get around the crashes.'

Dave furrowed his brow. 'The old Deeside Line was pulled up years ago. It is now a walking route. Trains haven't run for years. Well, except for the preservation society at the Royal

Deeside Railway, opposite Crathes Castle. There are a few yards of line departing from the Victorian replica Railway Station.'

'Tell your boys and girls to get their running shoes on. I'll ride shotgun in the Land Rover, Jason will drive. You take the rear with Sabre. I'll soon have you all out of here and to safety. Go have your talk. We've someone to collect first.'

Chapter 16

'I'm glad we aren't breaking the news about their families to the teenagers,' sighed Jason as he and Imo drove past the smouldering Guide hut.

Imo stuck her head through the vehicle's window. 'Smells like pork.'

Jason lifted one eyebrow as he steered them through the car park and slowed for the grass verge. Driving around the edge of the arena, he scanned the exhibitors they hadn't checked. They'd relied on the drone's heat detection to alert them to any survivors or the infected.

'Stop!' yelled Imo, opening her door, leaping out as the Land Rover skidded to a halt, throwing up four divots in the plush grass.

Jason dived out, grabbing his rifle from the back as he released Sabre. The dog ran to his mistress. Scanning the area, Jason watched as Imo ran towards a tent that boasted palm readings. She stopped short at a tall pole, set several feet away from the tent. On its slender frame were markings ranging from one to a hundred. A round metal object, like an old-fashioned school dinner bell, was proudly stuck at the top. Imo lifted a red, thick, wooden mallet with a long, wooden handle. She gave it several swings, then leant it against her legs.

Laughing, Jason declared, 'This area is an old Victorian Fayre. That's the High Striker. You test your strength and try to hit the hammer bell at the top. If the stallholder took a dislike to you or wanted to embarrass you, he'd surreptitiously tighten the ratchet at the back of the frame. It gave it more resistance so you couldn't reach the top.'

'Let's have a try!' Imo spat on her hands, rubbed them, and hoisted the mallet over her head and sent it crashing down on the peg on the ground. The spring-loaded lever rushed up and rang the bell next to the King's crown. 'Bingo!'

'Wrong game. But well done.' He slung his rifle over his shoulder and took the offered hammer. Levelling over the peg, he raised the hammer up and down a few times and then drove it home. The lever raised a few inches, like an alcoholic's flaccid penis being teased by a one-night stand.

Imo whistled a tune as she discreetly removed her hand from the back of the frame. 'I win!' she boasted.

Scratching his head, Jason looked up and down the frame. 'It looks harder than I thought it would be.'

They nudged shoulders, staring at the one hundred marker on the test your strength game.

Behind them, a black greying hand lifted the flap of the adjacent tent. A woman with jet black curly hair, wearing a long flowing velvet dress, crept out. Her wheezing, rasping breath was unheard above the sound of Imo teasing Jason on her win. Standing up, she let go of several brown cards that looked like she had stained them with thin gravy. Illustrated on them were dancing people. She gripped one card, whose harlequin costumed figure held a scythe. Behind this painted character was a ghoul in draping cloth, hood over his bending head, arms stretching out and encased in his dull fabric. A tiny treasure chest laid open at their feet was spilling gold coins beside a bejewelled crown. The woman clutched this card tighter and slunk to the duo, dragging her ankle, which was twisted to one side, like she was playing hockey. Arms held aloft; she was an inch from Imo's throat, dirt-ridden fingers splayed, nails sharpened like talons on an eagle.

Twisting around, arms above her head, Imo slammed the hammer home onto the woman's head. Driving it down, she laughed at the sound of crushing bone. Blood flooded out, running down the squashed face, turning her dull features a bright red. It mixed with yellowing, oozing brain matter. Imo shouted out, 'Strike! One hundred!'

Rolling his eyes, Jason stooped and picked up the tarot card the dying woman was clasping. A skeleton, grinning teeth from its bare skull, was sweeping a scythe across a dusty field. La Mort was printed below the fearsome figure.

Chapter 17

'The stupid bitch,' shouted Imo, a curl on her lips.

'Who, this fortune teller? I've never believed in all that stuff. Pippa did. Just a laugh, really. I wonder if she foretold her own death?'

Imo dug deep into a pouch and took out a small pair of binoculars. She peered across the arena. 'Look at who's swaying from the monster truck.'

Jason lifted his rifle and looked through the optics, his eyes narrowing as the gun's sights focused on a swinging figure. 'Oh, Christ!' he yelled. The rifle moved up and then down. 'The rope is too thin, it'll snap, but not before she's fully hung herself. She's choking but making no effort to escape from the cord biting into her neck.' His finger tightened on his trigger. As he breathed out, he muttered, 'You don't get an easy way out after your sins, Hazel.' He pulled the trigger, sighted again, shifting his aim slightly, and released another single bullet.

Across the arena, the figure, hanging by a thin, blue rope, taken from the exploded corpse of a bull, jiggered. Its neck twisting as the bullet frayed the cord. Then another bullet sliced through the rope. The line was severed, and Hazel fell to the grass, her body laid still in its sprawled state.

Jason ran, rifle held by his side, other arm pumping himself forward.

Imo shrugged at Sabre and sauntered over, swinging her hammer around. Flecks of blood flew from it.

Sabre ran forward, sniffing and then licking the crimson grass blades.

Skidding to a halt, Jason rolled Hazel onto her back, straightening her limbs. He began pumping on her chest, curses flying from his lips. Spittle flew on Hazel's chest as he pounded on it, recalling the first aid training from his time in the RAF Regiment. Craning his neck forward, he sealed his lips over hers and gave her two quick breaths, watching her chest rise and fall. He shouted more oaths as he placed his hands over her sternum, straightened his arms, and pumped up and down.

'Forget it, Cowboy. She's dead. Probably snapped her neck. Even if you saved her, she'd have spinal cord damage.'

'What the fuck do you know?' Jason yelled as he counted to thirty.

'On the wing, in prison, some girls got desperately unhappy. I've seen a few hangings.' Imo puffed out her cheeks then stuck her tongue out, tilted her head to the side and back and mimicked pulling a tight rope above her head. 'The screws could never revive them. Except one. She came back seven months later after spending time on a rehabilitation ward, learning how to wheel a chair and put a tube inside herself to urinate. The authorities made her finish her year sentence despite being sentenced to a disability for life.'

Ignoring her, Jason took a deep breath, knelt over her mouth, and pumped in valuable air. Hazel was deathly still as Jason felt her pulse on her wrist and neck. Placing his hands over her breastbone, he pumped down, counting in rhythm.

Air escaped Hazel's open mouth. She spat out and rasped. Her eyelids lifted.

Above her, Imo poised with her hammer, fingers white as she grasped the handle in anticipation. Jason thrust away her arm. 'What the actual fuck!' exclaimed Imo. 'What if she comes back as a zombie?'

Jason, unable to help himself, knelt and prised Hazel's eyes open. He felt pressure, and her eyeballs moved to his left. 'She's alive!' he whispered in awe, mouth agape. He moved her onto her side, feeling resistance.

'Leave me alone,' croaked Hazel, feeling under her hoodie material for her neck.

'You are lucky. The rope was wrapped around your thick hood and slipped. I shot it in time.'

Hazel took two deep breaths as she felt around her body. 'I don't deserve to be rescued. Let me take my chances with the zombies or find another rope.'

'Yes. You don't deserve to be rescued. But you have been. You are responsible for Raven's death. You must live with that for the rest of your life. But we are giving you the chance to redeem yourself. That's why I shot your rope.'

'How?' Hazel's brow furrowed.

'We have a hall of Scouts waiting to be rescued. They need someone to watch their backs as they make their way to safety. It's up to you if you go with them or remain here and get attacked. Get killed or save others from being killed. It's time to make amends.'

'Raven is all I can think of.'

'Good. She deserves to be remembered. Her family is probably dead. She tried to prevent her Rainbows from killing others. Raven should never be forgotten.'

Hazel sat up, looking at the end of the rope dangling from the gap between the monster truck's doorframe and the edge of the wheel. She took the frayed end of the rope hanging from her neck and tried to tighten it.

Imo dropped her hammer, unsheathed her knife, and cut away the rope from Hazel's neck while staring into her face. 'No red eyes. Shame.' Sheathing her knife, she threw the cord behind her. 'Time to atone. We need your help. Follow us. We've some transport to prepare.'

Chapter 18

Imo climbed up the grass bank, leapt over the wooden fence, and ran across the road. Sabre ran alongside her, relishing the exercise. Stopping at a large pane of glass, Imo raised her hammer and struck the window. Her new weapon bounced back, and she yelled out in pain as red-hot pokers ran up her arms. Dropping the handle, shaking her arms, she cursed as she danced on the street.

Supporting Hazel as she wheezed at the effort of their climb, Jason told her to wait by the kerb. He walked up to Imo and gently led her back a few steps, making sure the dog followed her. Raising his rifle, he aimed at the enormous window. 'You'll never learn! I'll gain us entry.' As he tightened his finger on the trigger, a figure stepped in front of his arc of fire, walked to the adjacent door, and opened it.

Imo's hand flew to her forehead. 'That's no fun!'

'But it is cleaner,' retorted Hazel.

'I could have shot you!' warned Jason.

Hazel shrugged, then winced at the pain coming from her throat. 'Would it have mattered?' Stepping into the shop, the smell of rubber assailed her. It was mixed with a metallic twang. Strung from the walls were various bicycle wheels, tools, saddles, puncture repair kits, and rubber tubes. Further back from the till area were rows of bikes held in special frames. Mountain and racer models of varying height.

Jason grinned. 'They'll get around any obstacle with these. Their fit legs will soon crunch the miles and get them to safety.'

'I'd love to see the look on the colonel's face when twenty-odd Scouts rock up at the fence.'

Looking around, Hazel scratched her head. 'I don't understand. Why do you need me?'

'You work with trucks. Had a tyre lever. I reckon you can soon get these measured up for each Scout and roadworthy. Adjust the handlebars, make sure the tyres are sound, that sort of thing. I need you to lead them to safety.'

'Haven't they a leader?'

'Yes. His bike will need a basket in front. For his weapons. He'll be protecting their rear.'

'Oh. Yes. Okay.' Running her hands along the frame of a mountain bike, Hazel tried a smile, her neck muscles straining hard as she looked up. 'I can help them get home?'

'To safety. Perhaps you can leave with them,' Jason encouraged, head nodding. 'Build a new life for yourself. Help others. Do good for the rest of your life? It's a precious gift.'

He tore off a sheet of paper at the till area and wrote an address down.

Hazel mirrored his nodding. A tentative 'Yes' escaped her pursed lips. Reaching down, she patted Sabre on his head.

'Good. Start by going here. To my wife, Pippa, and her parents. Describe what you've seen. Tell her I am okay,' his voice broke. Coughing, he explained, 'She needs to know Imogen and I are doing our duty. Tell her about rescuing the Scouts, and you.'

Nodding eagerly, 'Yes. I shall tell her how you saved me.' Lowering her eyes, 'Thank you.'

Imo curtsied. 'You're welcome!' she gleefully exclaimed, clutching her hammer like Thor.

Grinning, Jason grabbed the nearest bicycle from its rack and passed it to Hazel. 'We'll secure the stockroom and the staff rooms to make sure it is safe for you. It'll be dark soon. Do you want to spend the night in your truck or at the Scout hut?'

'I'll stay here and work until I've made ready about thirty bikes and gathered helmets and other supplies.' Scanning the shelves, she added, 'There are plenty of torches and batteries. I'll place them on the floor and on the shelving. It should give me enough lighting to go by. Please let me do this.'

Jason glanced from her to around the shop, looking for anything sharp or ropes, and asked directly. 'Promise me you'll do it and not take your life? There are about thirty souls relying on you.'

'I promise. I won't let you, or them, down.' Squatting, she flung her arms around Sabre and clinched him.

'Okay. When we leave, lock the door, and don't open it for anyone except us.' Looking at them both, 'We'll leave Sabre with you. For company and protection. We'll bring the Scouts to you at first light.' Taking what food and drink he had from his pouches, nodding for Imo to do the same. He suggested, 'There may be some food and drink in the staff room, perhaps even a comfortable chair to sleep on. We'll have a look as we clear the building.' Walking to the door, he pulled it shut and turned the lock. He gave it a few tugs, satisfying himself that the infected probably wouldn't be able to get through it.

Imo reluctantly parted with her stolen chocolate. 'There better be more on the shelves when we get out of here. I'm not spending the night without my chocolate hit,' she muttered. 'Bad enough I'm losing my best friend until the morning.' Narrowing her eyes, she hissed to Hazel, 'You'd better look after my boy.'

Hearing her whinging, Jason rolled his eyes. 'We'll go shopping in a minute. You can even get Sabre a treat for the morning. Let's check the storerooms and office.'

'Doubt there'll be sweeties there,' she grumbled, following through the back doorway.

A short passageway led to stairs and another door. Seeing the key in the lock, Jason turned it and poked his head out. There was a backyard, a high wall secured the area from all sides. Three chairs and a metal outdoor table were the only items on the slabbed patio that stretched from wall to wall. Enough for each member of staff. One or two were smokers, judging by the bucket filled with sand and cigarette stubs between two chairs. He returned to Imo. 'Nothing. Look, if we encounter any infected, we should go for silent kills. We don't want to distress Hazel anymore. It'll spook her having to spend the night with corpses. Can you manage that?'

Imo grinned and raised her hammer, giving it a kiss. 'It'll be my pleasure!'

Sighing, then grimacing when he saw the dried blood she was puckering up to, Jason wondered why he'd even bothered to ask. He led the way up the stairs, treading as lightly as he could, slinging his rifle, and taking out his combat knife from its sheath. He gulped as the natural light left the windowless upper landing. Squinting his eyes, he made out a doorway to his right, felt for a handle, and pushed it open.

Chapter 19

Skylights that extended across the roof flooded the vast room with the last of that evening's sunlight. Rows and rows of brand-new bicycles stretched from end to end, four columns deep. 'There must be tens of thousands of pounds of stock here,' marvelled Jason. Thrusting his knife in the air at a swarm of flies hovering around him, he was relieved to see most of them fly off and out of the open doorway.

'My uncle would have his friends and their vans here within the hour if he'd stumbled across this lot. He'd even have those boxes over there.' Imo lifted her hammer across to the far wall where neat piles of boxes were stacked upon each other like an OCD Lego maker had been building a wall. Each were labelled with their contents in large marker pen writing. None contained food or drink.

Imo lowered her hammer and tutted. 'No zombies, darling,' she whispered seductively to her hammer. 'Maybe later.'

Rolling his eyes, he asked sardonically, 'Named it, yet?' Not waiting for a witty reply, Jason pointed with the blade of his knife to the other corner. A glass fronted office, with an open door, lay ahead. 'I'll go first, you follow.'

'Yeah, no chance,' challenged Imo, stepping ahead of him and running into the room, her boots clomping across the bare wooden floorboards. Drawing to a halt, she shouted at the figure curled in a ball, back facing her, on a battered black leather sofa.

Waiting for a response, she shrugged her shoulders when Jason joined her.

He stretched out his arm, palm uppermost at the figure, inviting her to approach what looked like a young man. His short brown hair was poking out from under a tartan blanket.

Nudging him gently with the edge of her hammer, Imo shouted, 'Wake up, fella!'

Waiting a few seconds for a response, she then used the hammer to poke under the blanket, hook it, and then whipped it off the prone figure. 'Fuck! Look at him!' she marvelled. 'He looks like an Egyptian mummy! Or is it a daddy?'

Jason stepped forward. Retching as he stared back at the shrunken face that seemed wrapped as tight as clingfilm around his gaunt skull. Grinning teeth from shrivelled gums and crusted lips appeared to mock them when Imo flipped the body over. His exposed arms looked like he'd been under a sun bed too long and had baked and then desiccated into dry husks. His skeletal hands were clasped together. A note was clamped around his withered fingers. Jason gently withdrew it.

'What's it say?' asked Imo, leaning down and staring back at the open eyes, opaque eyeballs staring sightlessly back. 'Does it give a clue to where the hidden treasure is, you know, like in the Tomb Raider films and video games?'

Jason tutted and read it aloud. 'I don't know what's happening. I'm too afraid to go outside. When I look through the windows, I can see people attacking each other and hear their screams, night after night. My phone won't work and the electric and water are off. I've left the doors unlocked because I've built this business from scratch and don't want to be vandalised. I was respraying a bike frame just before the violence started -'

'That'll explain how you survived,' Imo interrupted, talking to the corpse. 'I bet you had on one of those filter masks. The paint fumes can be toxic.' She shrugged. 'I did a lot of graffiti when I was younger. You should have seen my tag!'

Ignoring her, Jason carried on reading aloud. He wanted to learn more. 'I was working on my own. I love my shop and don't want looters smashing my windows and damaging my doors. They can take what they want. I'm insured. That's why the doors are unlocked. I ran out of food four days ago and have nothing else to drink.' Jason paused, glancing at the nearby table, and saw only two small, drained bottles of water and an empty noodle pot, a fork sitting in the plastic container. 'I'm writing this five days after the attacks began. I'm feeling weak and am going to sleep now. My parents live at,' Jason skipped the address, knowing his family was likely to be dead. 'He signed it Jamir.'

Imo stepped away from the corpse. 'Poor sod. There probably wasn't much to him before the attack. He starved to death. Looks like he was also dehydrated. A cruel way to go. No wonder he looks so thin and frail. Shrivelled up in a ball.'

Jason leaned forward and closed Jamir's eyelids. The skin flaked apart as he pulled them down, exposing the eyeballs. A maggot wiggled free from one. Bile rose in Jason's throat, and he swallowed hard. Pulling the blanket back over the body, he whispered, 'Go in peace, Jamir.' Looking around, he spied a wall-mounted television, a gaming console with a pile of games and three controllers. Two large speakers were mounted on either side of the room. 'He must have been great friends with his work colleagues. Looks like a right bachelor pad in here. I don't want Hazel looking through the windows and seeing Jamir. Give me a hand, please, Imo. We'll turn the sofa against the wall to shield him, then lock the door and keep the key. I'll advise her not to go into the room.'

Imo eased the sofa across. 'Jamir must have weighed next to nothing.' Black sludge oozed out of the torn lining from the back of the sofa.

Stepping around it, Jason gave one final push and ran to the other door.

Imo heard a toilet lid being slammed against a tiled wall and the familiar sound of vomiting. 'Don't take it personally, Jamir. He does that to everyone we find.' She adjusted his body, so it was better shielded from view.

Wiping his mouth with the sleeve of his combat jacket, Jason rasped, 'Bathroom is clear. I opened the window to get rid of some of those damned flies that are hanging around.' Running his tongue around his dry mouth, he croaked, 'Some tastes and smells linger.' He wrinkled his nose. Waving his hands around, he swotted at several of the more persistent flies. 'Grab a bike suitable for a Scout leader. We may as well return to Hazel fully laden. I don't want her coming up here and chancing upon Jamir.' He pulled down a racing bike from a rack and wheeled it out of the door.

Imo heard him bump it down the stairs, stop and then the creak of the door to the patio area. 'No flies on him!'

Chapter 20

Pulling out his comms earpiece, Jason unfurled his cable and placed the unit on the till counter. 'You can contact us with this. Imo will be listening. We can be here within the minute. This road and the one to the Scout hut are easily passable.'

Watching Imo whisper something into the dog's ear, Hazel asked, 'Would you prefer to take the dog with you?'

'No,' replied Jason, adamantly. 'I don't think you are up to firing weapons. Sabre will keep guard over you and protect you. If you don't want him toileting in here, there is a backyard through there.' Pointing to the doorway, he warned, 'Don't go upstairs.'

Gulping, she looked wide-eyed.

He explained, 'It's not safe. The floorboards are thin. Some have gaping holes.'

Her shoulders dropped as she let out a held breath.

'Do you think you've enough equipment and tools down here to get all thirty bikes roadworthy?'

Nodding, she asked, 'Where should I go for a toilet?'

'Ah,' Jason replied, red-faced. 'The toilet upstairs isn't useable, it's full of sick.'

'Yuck!' she exclaimed.

Rubbing Sabre's fur, Imo teased, 'Yeah, I wonder what dirty bastard did that?'

Rummaging around behind the till, Jason came away with a metal bin. He pushed down pieces of paper in it. 'This'll do you. The paper will absorb the liquid and smell. There is a box of tissues on the shelf under the till.' Reaching into a pouch, he withdrew a packet of personal wipes he'd requisitioned from a shop. 'In case you need a wash. Lemon scented,' he added, helpfully.

'He carries them, so he provides a fruity blow job for any lady friends he meets.' Imo raised her arms aloft, widened her mouth and acted like a zombie, sticking her tongue on and off the side of her cheek.

Hazel tittered as Jason went redder. 'Yes, well, I'll just take Sabre for a toilet. It'll save you going outside later. Though those brick walls are high enough to deter most people.' Whistling, he grabbed his rifle and opened the shop door. A furry shape darted out and made for the nearest lamppost.

'Seriously, though. Keep alive and fix those bikes.' Lifting her hammer above her head, Imo muttered, 'I expect my boy to be in one piece when I get back.'

Nodding violently, then shuddering at the sound of a rifle shot, she arched her eyebrows. 'You wouldn't dare do anything to me. Not while Jason is here.'

Stretching forward, arms lowering, Imo spotted the flashing light on the shop's CCTV camera above the till. 'Of course not,' she smiled. 'We've got to keep you alive. In fact, I don't think you should be worried about the dark. The fuckwit of a colonel will switch the lights on soon.'

Hazel's head cocked. 'What colonel?' She looked at the door. 'Is he your senior officer?'

Flicking her head toward the door, 'Maybe his, but not mine. I'm a free woman. Well, in Aberdeenshire at least.'

The fluorescent tube above them made three ticking noises, flickered, and sprang on, beaming down on them.

'Don't you worry about alerting me to danger. I've a feeling you'll be watched over.'

Hazel looked nervously around, then beamed as Sabre came bounding in, followed by Jason, a rifle in one hand, and a carrier bag in the other. He placed it on the counter. 'A few goodies and drinks from the shop next door. To keep you and Sabre here going.'

'Don't be feeding my boy chocolate. It's lethal to dogs,' warned Imo.

'Let's get going. We've some Scouts to organise.' Turning to Hazel, 'Remember, they are relying on you. Lock this door as soon as we leave. Open it only for us.'

Hazel nodded, reached for Sabre's ear to tickle and felt fresh air. The dog was being cuddled by Imo, and she was sure she saw tears falling from the woman.

Chapter 21

Running up the High Street, Imo raised her hammer as she leapt and brought it down on the head of an infected woman feeding on a corpse outside a kebab shop. She rained blow upon blow as she shattered its skull. Yellow and red mush flew in all directions, along with bone shards, then teeth.

Looking down as he approached, Jason asked, 'Pissed off?'

Breathlessly swinging her hammer, Imo shouted, 'Fuck off, I'm busy working.'

'It's about Sabre, isn't it?'

'No,' she retorted, like a petulant child. Walking away, she booted open the nearest shop door. Walking into the florist, she glanced around, looking for items to add to her cache.

'Need a bouquet for your boy?' teased Jason, walking in.

'Bugger off. He's my dog to give. She's suicidal. She's a liability. Let her off herself.'

Taking her by the shoulder, turning her gently around, 'That's exactly why she has him. We need to protect the uninfected. She won't harm herself while she has him to look after. Or rather, him to look after her. She'll fuss over him between fixing bikes. I found some dog brushes in the shop. She will feed him well and groom him. Besides,' he continued, pulling out a flower from the nearest withered boutique. 'You always have me!' He presented her with a wilted rose whose petals crumbled to dust as he held it up to her nose.

Smiling, she took the wilted stem. 'I've never had flowers before.'

'What! Never?' he exclaimed.

Shaking her head, 'My boyfriends were more my suppliers, really. They got what they wanted, and I got what I needed from them.'

'Oh, sorry.'

'Don't be. It's a period of my life I'm not proud of, but don't mind admitting and talking about and only have fleeting memories of, now and again. Mostly in my dreams.'

'Should we head back to the Land Rover? You probably need your methadone?'

'Yes, please. I like to have it close by and need to time my dosages carefully. It stops me from slipping. I don't want to be that person again. There are too many chemists with open doors and shelves, in the towns and villages we are evacuating.'

Taking her hand, 'I think we are both different people now. This mission has reshaped us.'

Relishing his warmth, she allowed herself to be led outside and down the High Street and past the ice-cream kiosk.

Entering the park, they looked like a courting couple enjoying a romantic walk during a late-summer evening. The setting sun dipped below the trees as they took their seats in their Land Rover, Imo wistfully looking in the back for her furry friend. She wiped her eyes as Jason sped off.

Puffing his chest out, the colonel addressed his second-in-command. 'Flight Sergeant, revise your rota for that sector. Minimum staff only until first light, then all hands on deck. I want everyone on duty and refreshed. Those Scouts are going to make it to the fence in one piece.'

'Sir,' acknowledged his second-in-command, smiling at the correct use of his rank. Reaching for a pen, he began scribbling away at the form on his desk, putting his name first for a meal break and some shut eye.

Jason banged on the Scout hut door and peered through the window. He watched Dave reach for the tomahawk he had slotted through his belt, then relax his grip when he saw the enormous bag the flight sergeant carried. Jason knew the food and drink he and Imo had pilfered from the shops he'd driven around would be gratefully received with no questions asked by the Scouts.

Opening the door for them both, Dave asked, 'Where's the dog? Is he okay? Has the poor thing been hurt?'

'He's with a friend.'

'The one you went to collect. What happened?'

'The transport will have to wait until the morning. It's too dangerous to travel in the dark.' Passing the bag, Jason added, 'There are enough rations to feed everyone this evening and in the morning. I want everyone to have used the toilet and eaten their fill as soon as the sun comes up. They'll need their energy.'

Grabbing the bag, looking inside with eyes alight, the Scout Leader, turned to go.

'How did your talk go?' Jason grimaced. 'Daft question. Sorry. It can't have been easy, telling your troop their families are probably dead.'

Twisting back, 'No, it wasn't. Especially telling my son his sister and mother, my daughter and wife, have been killed.' Dave's eyes filled with tears.

'Shit. I didn't realise. Your son is here?'

Dave nodded. Swallowing a few times, he eventually trusted his voice. 'Austin is my boy. Thank the Lord, he made it through this nightmare. I couldn't have lost him, too. He's busy showing off the Glock 19 to his friends. Don't worry, he's a better firearms expert than I am. It's part of his high-functioning Asperger's. A love for all things military. That's why he took such a shine to Imo. His mum was much better than me in managing him in the early days. He responds better to women. His love of scouting comes from that fascination too, uniform and discipline.'

Jason placed his hand on the man's shoulder and squeezed it. 'You've done well. Tomorrow, you will lead them to safety and build a new life with your boy.'

'What happens to you? Both of you?'

'We stay here. Rescue more people, hopefully. Or end the suffering of the infected. I'll give you an address later. Perhaps you can visit it with Austin. Pippa will be there. My wife. She'd love to meet him.'

'It seems we are both to be deprived of our wives. I pray you'll get to see her soon.'

'He will,' declared Imo, as she joined them, hefting a bag brimming with bottles. 'All fizzy pop and full of additives, but it'll make a change from boiled water. I grabbed as many sugar-free ones for those with ADHD. We want some sleep tonight,' she joked, locking the door behind her. 'I don't want any Scouts running around the hall. We had enough of that with the Guides.'

The main hall door swung open, and Austin immediately pointed to their Land Rover, backlit in the dying sun. 'Cor, that's a GPMG. I've only ever seen those on YouTube. Can I go outside and see it close up?'

His father blocked his way. 'No, Austin, remember our conversation about staying safe? In the hut?'

'Without mum and Willow?' he said dead-panned.

'That's right,' encouraged Dave, tears falling.

'I'll get back in the hall. Here, I've counted the bullets for you and reloaded. Seven. You'll need a fresh magazine.' He handed his father the Glock 19, butt first.

'Thank you, Austin. Now gather the troop. Tell them we have fresh food and drink to enjoy.' Spying the cans of deodorant and wet wipes, 'And tell them to perform field hygiene first. Then after our meal, we'll get some sleep.'

Austin nodded once and turned to Imo. 'I've put a spare sleeping bag next to mine. You can bed down there.'

'Okay, sunshine, but no funny business!' teased Imo.

Austin looked at her with his dead-pan face and tilted his head.

Laughing, Jason slapped her on the shoulder. 'You've just been blown off.'

'That's more than you'll be getting tonight, Cowboy. Even if you had lemon scented wet wipes.'

Chapter 22

Having stood guard for the second watch, Imo went around the hall, shaking awake the Scouts and their leader. She left Jason to last. Throughout the night, she'd silently endured their stinking flatulence and had cradled one or two who had cried out for their mothers in their sleep. Periodically she had gone to the front door and peered through the glass to the High Street in the pretence of looking for the infected. Her gaze was directed to the bicycle shop each time.

Stretching, then grabbing his boots, Jason laced them up and was on his feet, rifle in hand. A tin mug filled with instant coffee was passed to him. 'Thanks, Skip. What I'd give for a proper coffee.'

'It's the least I can do. To get my troop to safety. To get Austin away from the infected. I can't imagine my wife and daughter being like that. I hope their end was quick.'

Hands full, Jason mumbled, 'Sorry, mate.'

Dave turned, wiping at his eyes, looking for Austin.

Sensing his need, Jason raised his mug toward the doorway. 'He's with Imo. Even woke up during her watch and kept her company.'

'An unlikely pairing. As are you both? I'm surprised she's in the military. Doesn't seem the type.'

Jason didn't correct him as he left to find his son.

The Portakabin door swung open and several operators, dressed in military fatigues, marched in. They took their places behind terminals. Screens lit up. Coffee thermoses were placed carefully alongside mouses and keyboards.

The colonel watched each of his team settle in their seats. His narrowed eyes going from one to the other. Not a word was spoken. They exchanged no military banter. 'Any movement from the Scout hut?' he barked at the nearest camera operator as he saw her scroll with her mouse.

'I've tapped into the nearest lamppost CCTV, sir. It's been recording all night. There was no movement.'

'Good. I want them alive. I need the numbers. Keep monitoring.'

'How will you get us all safely to the transport?' asked Dave, squinting at Imo's uniform, trying to spot an insignia or rank badge.

'I think the least fit of you can go in the back of the Land Rover, then the others can run behind. Or we can make several trips. Either Jason or I will be in the back, providing covering fire, if needed.'

As his father was talking to Imo, Austin tiptoed around them, edging to the front door. Under his breath he marvelled, 'A 7.62 belt with up to seven-hundred and fifty rounds.' He silently unlocked the front door and stepped out into the August early dawn. Dew drops glistening away in the grass by the totem pole caught his gaze. Then he strode towards the Land Rover. As he was climbing the tailgate, a figure dashed forward, springing onto him. It knocked Austin to the ground. The Scout screamed, a monotone, elongated cry of surprise.

The figure grabbed at his Scout muffler, wrapping the cloth around Austin's neck, tightening it, choking off the scream.

'That is my son!' exclaimed Dave, running to the door, right hand shooting down to his belt. Seeing the roaring figure of a man constricting the scarf, Dave unclasped his leather pouch and withdrew his tomahawk. 'Stay down, Austin!' he warned. It sailed through the air and embedded itself in the base of the skull of the attacking man. The infected attacker shuddered and fell forward, face on the dirt as Austin rolled away.

Leaping to his feet, he wandered back to the Land Rover. 'A C2 optical sight,' he murmured, rubbing at his throat, unfurling his muffler. Looking down at the garment, he realised his woggle was missing. Returning to the corpse, he felt underneath the still body, retrieved it, and slid his muffler through its hole. He carefully tightened the scarf, glimpsed back at the body, and asked, 'Shall I retrieve your tomahawk, Skip?'

Hands shaking, walking to his son, then wrapping his arms around him, Dave replied in a faltering voice, 'Let's leave it where it is, son. I'll get another from the Leader's room.' He led his son back to the safety of the hut, turning once to look at the corpse.

Imo looked on thoughtfully and wondered about putting one boot on the back of the man's neck and heaving out the formidable weapon. Instead, she raised her hammer, looking around in disgust. It was a solitary attack. As she, too, returned to the hut, she gave a wistful look up the hill.

A round of applause cracked through the tense atmosphere of the HQ like thunder after a hot summer week. Operators looked from one to the other, smiling. One gave a low whistle of appreciation. 'Some throw!' exclaimed another.

'That's enough!' bellowed the colonel as he made a mental note to arrange for the Scout Leader to give a teaching session to his squadron after this mission was complete.

'I'm sorry. Austin doesn't understand personal danger like we would. He gets fascinated and lost in a subject. He needs close monitoring.' Dave's hands were shaking as he pointed outside.

'No bother,' replied a cheerful Imo. 'That was some kill. Best you re-arm yourself. Hazel has somewhere to stow your weapons. You'll need lots of them.' She hesitated momentarily, summing up whether to ask for one. She decided he needed them more. Scooping up her shotgun in her free hand, she told Dave, 'Get the door. I'll secure the area.' Imo strode outside and walked off, out of view.

Jason stood at the doorway, watching her go around the building, then crossing the road and looking up and down the street. She spent longer looking up.

Handing Jason her comms unit, 'Safe. Let's get underway. See if Hazel's been good to her word.'

'Thanks, Imo.' Jason turned to Dave. 'No equipment needed. Get your least fit Scouts crammed into the back of the Land Rover. Leave room for me to get behind the big gun. The rest of you can run behind us. Imo will drive slowly.

A couple can cram in the front seat but tell them not to obscure Imo's view to the left.'

'Austin, you go first. You'll not be able to keep up.' Dave watched him go back outside, craning his neck left and right at the door until his son was standing to the left of the mighty looking weapon. He ushered a dozen more of the young Scouts outside, grateful to see Imo circling around the vehicle, her eyes constantly scanning the area. He watched as Jason suddenly knelt, looked through his rifle's sights, and the Scout Leader shuddered as he heard a single shot. The flight sergeant stood and joined Imo in scanning the area.

'I'm scared, Skip,' wailed a trembling Scout, biting his lip to stop himself from crying.

Adjusting his belt, heavily laden with tomahawks, the Scout Leader took the young boy's hand. 'Be brave. Run beside me. Don't look around. Keep your eyes on the Land Rover. We'll be safe soon.'

The battered Land Rover spluttered and rumbled into life, its exhaust belching in protest at the extra weight. Jason jumped on board and made to make ready the GPMG as Imo drove away. It surprised him to look down to see Austin expertly feeding in the link belt and opening a fresh ammo box. As he lowered his arched eyes, he placed his hand to his ear, listening to the comms spring into life. Looking at the running troop of Scouts and the wheezing Scout Leader, Jason cried, 'Fuck!'

Chapter 23

'Say again, sir,' shouted Jason, not believing the information. He wished Imo had her comms, so he could double-check the report.

'Sixty heat signatures heading your way,' confirmed the colonel as Imo turned right into the High Street. 'Running fast,' added the officer.

Jason banged twice on the roof of the Land Rover's cabin.

Skidding to a halt, Imo threw her young charges to the floor of the Land Rover. Grabbing her hammer and shotgun. 'Stay here,' she ordered.

'Stay down,' shouted Jason to his young charges. He jumped between them and stopped at the edge of the tailgate, bellowing to the Scout Leader. 'Take cover in the nearest shop. Bolt the doors if you can. Find a room you can lock. I'll give the all clear password of Wizards. Don't come out for anything or anyone else. We've got incoming. I'll protect the boys here.'

'But my son,' gasped Dave as he reached the Land Rover, arm outstretched.

'Just do it. There's no time. Boys, cover your ears with your hands or put your fingers in them. It's about to get noisy. Close your eyes.'

As Dave turned away, it did not surprise him to see Austin pull out a fresh link belt in preparation. Inhaling deeply, he shouted at his charges to follow him as he pushed open the door of the nearest shop. Ignoring the rows of spectacles, he counted as each young lad ran past him, joining the huddle at the rear of the store. Slamming the door tight, he snibbed the lock and strode to the back and into another room. 'Follow me, boys, the first ten in here.' He marshalled them into a dark room with eye charts on the walls and a raised seat, like that on a starship's deck. Beside it was a machine that held a binocular-like device resting on a large arm. 'Only come out when you hear the word Wizards spoken by me, Jason, or Imo.' Patting the nearest Scout on the shoulder, 'Lock the door, if you can.' Not waiting for a reply, the Scout Leader dived through the doorway, pushing open the adjacent door.

The twitch in the colonel's eye returned as he heard the flight sergeant's update. Striding across to the other end of the Portakabin, he bellowed at the operator piloting a drone, 'Divert it. Now. To my sector. Arm those missiles.'

'No can do, sir,' replied the operator. 'I'm on a mission signed off by the air commodore herself.'

The twitch grew rapid, pulsing heavily. 'I don't care. Divert it.'

The operator kept his gaze on the screen. 'Sorry, sir. She gave me an express order.'

The colonel fumbled at his holster.

The operator felt a cold plastic tube placed on the side of his head. It pressed hard into his flesh, touching bone. Gulping down, he stared hard at the screen as his hand moved the joystick to the left.

'What's up?' shouted Imo above the sound of Jason cocking the GPMG. She didn't think she'd have missed her comms unit. Her ear felt strangely empty without it. The feel of the wind around her earlobe left her bereft.

'We've incoming. HQ says about sixty. Body heat only. They've had no eyes on them. Not sure if they are friendly. The Scouts on foot are hiding in the opticians. The rest are shielding in the Land Rover.'

Imo winked at Austin. 'Remember your weapons drills, young lad. They might come in useful.'

Austin stared back, no emotion on his face. 'I'm ready.'

Looking ahead, Imo grinned. 'Good, because here they come, and I don't think I need contact lenses to see they are not friendly.' She rested her hammer on the bonnet. Pumping a fresh cartridge into her shotgun, she knelt out of the way of the GPMG fire and away from the casings she knew would come flying to its right.

Jason's mouth dropped as he saw the group swarm down the narrow hill from their left. Shoulders scraping against the brickwork of the shops and their backyards as the infected fought to get in the lead. Some were carrying thick pieces of wood, others metal piping, bricks, and large stones. One snarling woman had a large kitchen knife. 'I was right. They have learned to arm themselves.' Twisting the GPMG to his left, Jason fired, watching in horror as bodies twisted with the impact of the heavy calibre rounds. It shredded abdomens open, guts flopped out and the infected trod and slid about. Two men were cut in half, almost like they'd been sliced open by a charging cavalryman. Bullets tore clean through some and burst through the people behind, cutting down legs, severing limbs.

Imo stood, leaning over the bonnet, watching as Jason went to work, finally showing her why he'd earned his military stripes. Giving out an excited yell, she shouted, 'Save some fuckers for me!'

Her voice was lost to Jason above the sound of the roaring machine gun. He thought only of the boys and his duty to save them from this marauding crowd. His imagination going wild at the thought of the infected tearing into innocent flesh. All thought of vomiting gone.

A heavy thud came from the gun and the dying screams of the infected filled the air, along with the thunderous bellows of the survivors as they ran to the Land Rover.

A quiet voice, in a monotone, confirmed what Jason knew. 'You're out of ammo, Flight Sergeant. And the gun has likely overheated. There is no spare barrel.' Austin passed Jason a Mills bomb. 'I've pulled the ring for you. Throw it further than me.'

'Shit!' exclaimed Jason, taking the pineapple shaped bomb and tossing it, overarm to the furthest infected. It landed amongst them, exploding, taking down a wall that buried a crawling man, trailing a line of seeping bowel. It minced three running infected as shrapnel from the detonated projectile tore into their flesh and bone. Their innards decorating the whitewash of a building like the spray can of a graffiti artist. 'Take them out, Imo. The gimpy is fucked.'

Rising with a grin, Imo leapt onto the bonnet, scanning the area. Leaping from the vehicle, she ran towards the screaming runners and fired. The leader flew back. An enormous crater appeared in her chest, revealing a shattered rib cage as her lungs flopped uselessly down into the cavity, bouncing up and down. Her falling body tripped two more runners who squelched into the swamp of blood, guts, and severed limbs. They went sliding forward like they were taking part in a fun and muddy red obstacle course.

Imo jumped back, laughing as she threw her shotgun onto the bonnet and grabbed her hammer. With two hands, she swung it into the air and pummelled down on the nearest moving skull, blasting apart the bone as the hammerhead reached concrete. Withdrawing the bloody stump of the hammer, she cursed as she saw she'd shattered the hammerhead. She changed her grip, twisted her fingers, and drove the remains of her weapon into a man's mouth who was about to hit her with a metal pipe. It dug deep and erupted out of the base of his neck, paralysing him instantly as blood poured down his back. Imo pushed him away, eyes twinkling at her handiwork. Turning to grab her shotgun, she gave a double-take as Austin passed it to her.

'I've reloaded it for you. Ready to fire.'

'Cheers!' she beamed, showing him her years of poor dental hygiene. Pushing him to the floor, she stood over him as she blasted away at another blood covered infected, the victim's ponytail thick with congealed blood. Her spectacles shattered, glass embedding itself deep into her eyes and cheeks. Her head snapped back, head-butting the eager man behind her. He dropped his plank of wood, dazed. Imo grinned as she blasted first one shin and then the other, watching as he fell onto a bloodied stump and then another. He took a few waddling steps before falling face first into the mushy carcasses that laid before him.

Jason rushed to the tailgate, stepping on a trembling Scout's hand. He leaned over the side and vomited, narrowly missing another Scout whose hands were clasped to his eyes.

Pointing to the store with no one at the window, Imo gleefully announced, 'They missed all the fun, hiding in there.' Pointing to the back of the Land Rover, 'And that lot lying down didn't see a thing. They might as well have gone to Specsavers!'

Chapter 24

Ears ringing, voice sounding muffled, fighting against the after-effects of firing the GPMG without ear protection, Jason shouted, 'The comms. I can't hear a thing.' He thrust the unit over to Imo. 'The colonel might have an update. There was fresh information coming in as they attacked. I couldn't hear all of it.'

Imo glanced at the earpiece. 'You better not have earwax. I'm not putting it in if you have.'

Jason waved his hands around his ears. 'I can't hear a thing.'

Imo smiled and mouthed random words, pretending to have a conversation with him.

'Give it a few minutes,' he yelled. 'My hearing will come back then.'

'Don't rush, Cowboy, your conversation is never that funny, anyway. Or riveting'

'Why do you call him Cowboy?' a soft voice asked, suddenly at her side.

'Jesus!' she exclaimed. 'You're like a ninja, you creepy little fucker.'

'He's a flight sergeant,' insisted Austin. 'Not a cowboy.'

'Loosen up, kid. Don't take things so literally.' She saw him squatting and poking amongst the pile of carcases with a long bayonet he'd found in the back of the Land Rover. Grabbing it from him, 'And give me that. What would your dad think?'

'Skip,' declared Austin. 'Where is our leader? He should be here.'

'Settle down, kid. You did well, feeding the gimpy and pulling on the grenades. You'll have earned another badge.' Looking at his sleeve, she wondered where it would have fitted.

Rubbing the earpiece on her sleeve, she slotted it into her ear and grimaced at the shouting voice. 'Calm the fuck down, dear. You'll give yourself a heart attack. We've been busy. Give us more ammo next time you restock the Landie.'

'No time. Take cover. You've incoming.'

'Newsflash, dickhead. We've dealt with them.'

'Newsflash, bitch. There's about three hundred heading your way from your north. Swarming in from the housing estate. Take cover. Immediately.'

Gulping and twisting around, pulling out her earpiece, Imo squinted. Drawing up her binoculars, she focused and saw the swarm. 'Fuck.' Running to the Land Rover, dragging Austin with her, she ordered the cowering Scouts, 'Get out. Run to the opticians. Find your leader. The codeword is Wizards.

Take cover. Hide. Go,' she yelled. 'And take this creepy fucker with you.' She pushed Austin in their direction.

Jason creased his brow as he watched the Scouts leap from the vehicle and run across the street. 'Where are they going?' he yelled.

Imo turned him around and drew the binoculars to his eyes.

Grasping them, Jason altered the focus and screamed, 'But we are out of ammunition.'

Imo grinned. 'I know, right? This is going to be so much fun!' She pulled out her catapult and placed it on the roof of the Land Rover cabin. Thrusting the shotgun to Jason's chest, she waited until he grasped it and then handed him five cartridges.

'That's all?' eyebrows lifting.

'Yup.' Tapping his sheathed knife, she grinned and shouted, 'It's hand to hand thereafter.' Pushing in her earpiece into her comms, she boasted, 'Only three hundred against me and him. I don't fancy their odds!'

Smiling, unnerving those around him with his expression, the colonel spoke softly into his comms. 'I said, take cover. You've incoming.' He pushed his Glock further against the sweating drone operator's head.

'We know. We've seen them. I've my catapult at the ready and a pocket of ball bearings.'

The colonel rolled his eyes. He spelt out his words in sharp syllables, like he was on the drill square and teaching inept recruits. 'Put them away. Take cover. You've incoming.'

'We know. We are waiting for them to get nearer.'

'Stop being stupid and listen. The incoming is from us. Take cover. We'll be firing, now.' He dug the pistol and twisted the barrel.

Imo grabbed her catapult, then seized Jason by the collar and pulled him from the vehicle, and they ran to the nearest shop. She pushed him through the doorway and held out her palm. Jumping back, she slammed home the door and ran towards the approaching horde. 'Sabre, I'm coming for you, my boy.'

Chapter 25

'Fire!' yelled the colonel. 'Bring it down on them.'

The drone operator gulped as he flicked open a covered switch and pushed the red button down. Letting out a pent-up breath, he watched the screen. The colonel's head appearing over his as they squinted together.

Imogen heard a crack of thunder and lightning above her, though the sky was clear when she looked up. It sounded like someone had detonated a stick of old-fashioned dynamite. Then a black object appeared, streaking through the air, trailing a line of cloudy smoke. Its tip was glowing, like a lit cigarette. She traced it, head snapping across as she followed its trajectory. An almighty explosion erupted way ahead of her and she ran into a sudden gust of air. Debris flying in all directions.

Pumping hard with her legs and arms, she sprinted like an Olympian, grateful that debris hadn't struck the bike shop. Bricks bounced on the road ahead and she saw chunks of flesh. Tattered clothing floated in the air as a dark cloud descended. Through it, figures jumped over rubble, tripping as they went. Some failed to rise, others burst through. Their heads snapped up as they spied Imo and raced to her.

'Bollocks!' she cried as she spied the bike shop, about a hundred yards ahead of her. Pleading into her comms, 'My boy! Don't fire near my boy!' Her thigh muscles screamed in protest and waves of agony burst through her muscles as she ploughed on.

A thunderous noise burst from overhead and wind gushed down, almost knocking her from her feet. Dust kicked up and swirled like a giant teaspoon was stirring dried tea leaves. She slewed to a halt as a helicopter burst from the sky, sinking at an angle in front of her. A giant of a figure was manning The General, the larger GPMG. She'd heard about this weapon amongst the other Call of Duty gamers in prison. Grasping the two handles, the behemoth pumped round after round into the emerging survivors. Brass casings bounced around the helicopter's floor and were spat out from the two open doorways.

The deafening noise made Imo clasp her ears, her fingers going white as they dug into her hair, as if seeking comfort or warmth. Coughing and spitting at the dust clouds, she tried to keep her mouth closed.

The gunner eased his hands from the enormous gun, turning to face her from the other side of the open hatchway, and bowed.

A mocking voice broke into Imo's earpiece, 'You're welcome!'

Grinning, Imo ran to the bike shop, middle finger extended at the waving goliath of a figure who was raising himself from his curtsy. She saw him reach over and pat the shoulder of another man dressed in military fatigues, standing by the hatchway. The helicopter rose, tilted, and sped away to the south.

Shoulder to the frame, she swore at the pain as, after two crashes against it, she shattered the wood, and the lock gave way. Rushing into the shop, ignoring the thirty bicycles neatly lined up, standing proudly on their own kickstands.

Cowering in the corner, hands wrapped tightly around Sabre, was Hazel. Her face was buried in the dog's fur and her shoulders were heaving.

Sabre gave an excited bark and struggled against the grip on him. Back paws scrabbling against the wood of the floor and front paws scratching at the bare arms of his captive.

Hazel let off a sharp, 'Ouch,' and released her grip, rubbing at her arms as red welts appeared.

'My Boy!' screamed Imo as she ran towards Sabre, knelt, and spread her arms.

Sabre scrambled at the wood, his legs working furiously in rhythm with the wagging of his tail. His yelping rose to a high pitch. Circling on the spot twice, he regained his balance and jumped onto Imo.

His mistress flew back, laughing and giggling like a toddler being tickled. Clasping him tight, whispering into his cocked ears, kissing them, relishing the sweet taste of his ear wax on her lips. Inhaling deeply, she drew in his scent and sighed happily as she exhaled. 'I've missed you. Don't ever leave my side again. Promise me.' Taking his neck on both sides, she drew her hands to his face, bringing his muzzle closer. Their noses touched. His wet, hers moist from crying. They remained touching nose to snout for several seconds.

'Get a room!' laughed Jason, walking in, grabbing the comms unit from the counter. 'It's just been one night.' Ignoring the raised middle finger, Jason walked around the neat rows of bikes, each with a helmet dangling from their frames. Lights and bicycle pumps were attached to most of them. A wicker basket sat on the front of the tallest bicycle and there were deep pannier satchels attached to the back.

Thrusting his arm out to a squatting Hazel, Jason helped her to her feet. 'Thank you. Well done. Please stay here, and we'll bring the Scouts to you. They still need you. I'd like you to lead them to the Aberdeenshire border, along the A90.' Having seen the helicopter fly off and the empty casings on the road, he revealed his thoughts. 'I doubt you'll have any of the infected bother you. Grab a map from the shelf over there and plan a route. Take the back roads.'

'Thirty-three point two miles,' whispered a voice behind Jason.

The flight sergeant jumped, then twisted around, drawing his Glock. Raising it at chest height, drawing down on Austin. 'Don't do that!' he exclaimed. 'I could have shot you.'

Rubbing Sabre's chest, Imo laughed. 'Creepy wee bastard, isn't he?' She snatched her earpiece out and left it dangling as Sabre reached up and licked inside her lobe.

Austin looked at the bicycles. 'It should take about two hours and fifty minutes, allowing for a ten-minute break.'

Hazel squinted at him. 'How does he do that? How does he know?'

Ticking Sabre's ears, Imo chuckled, 'Trust us, he knows.' Rising to her feet, she reached into a pouch and threw Sabre a long, bone-shaped biscuit. 'I saved this for you.'

Catching it, Sabre settled onto the floor and crunched down on it.

Walking to Hazel, looming over her, Imo demanded, 'Did you feed him? Groom him? Get all the matted blood out? How much sleep did he get? Has he had breakfast? Has he had his morning shit and piss?'

Hazel spluttered over her words, unable to get a coherent reply out.

'Leave the poor woman alone,' sniggered Jason. 'You can see Sabre is well. It's only been one night, for fuck's sake.'

Imo turned and squared up to him, eyeball to eyeball, standing on tiptoes. 'Just remember, Cowboy, he's my dog. No more giving him away.'

Jason took a step back, stamping home his boot to join the other. He threw up a smart salute. 'Message received and understood.' Finishing on a drawl, 'Ma'am.'

Thumping him on the shoulder, 'You can teach me how to salute when we've time, as payment for your crimes.' Grinning, 'Let's get these Scouts on the road.' Nodding to Austin, 'I'll be glad to offload him. He appears out of nowhere like a stage magician.'

'Wizards, the codeword is wizards,' corrected Austin, walking to the door. 'You need to come with me and say it to the Scouts so they can come out of their safe places.'

Rolling her eyes, whistling for Sabre, Imo marched across to Hazel. Placing a hand on each of her shoulders, she smirked, 'Saddle up, girl! Prepare for the ride of your life!'

Chapter 26

'I really am sorry about Raven. I won't stop feeling guilty about her.' Tears fell from Hazel's eyes.

'Good. You were a stupid bitch, and her death is your fault. I won't sugarcoat it like he does,' snarled Imo. Seeing the lines of Scouts sat on their saddles behind her, she softened her voice. 'But now is the time to make amends with whatever God you believe in. Get these children to safety.' She looked between the rows of teenagers, reduced to boys and girls in their collective fear. Each was constantly scanning the area. 'Listen to Skip. Trust his judgement and obey his orders.' Checking her Glock, she passed it to Hazel. 'It's fully loaded and ready to fire. Point and shoot. Just press back on the trigger, nice and slow. Hold the pistol with two hands if you can. Don't shoot while cycling. Stop, breathe calmly, then fire.'

Hazel took it, her hands trembling. Placing it in her front basket, alongside the puncture repair kits, tin of oil, and spare inner tyre tubes.

Rolling her eyes, Imo mouthed, 'God help them,' as she turned away, clucking for Sabre to follow her.

Stepping back, the colonel holstered his pistol. Narrowing his eyes, he hissed, 'Bring the drone back. Re-arm it. Track the Scouts. Be ready to fire again. Bring them home, alive. All of them.'

Turning, the colonel barked, 'Flight Sergeant, ensure this man obeys my orders.'

'Sir!' acknowledged the second-in-command. Waiting until his superior officer had left the Portakabin, he took out a mobile phone.

Sitting astride his bicycle frame, feet firmly planted on the road, Dave leant forward and gave the brakes two firm pumps. The bicycle rocked, metal clanged on metal as unsheathed tomahawks bounced around the panniers and the wicker basket. Whispering conspiratorially to Jason, 'It's been a while since I rode a bicycle. I would have been in my teens.'

'Don't worry, you'll soon remember. It's like learning to ride a -' Jason laughed. 'Well, you know what I mean. The Scouts and Hazel are relying on you. Keep them and your son safe.'

Thrusting out his left hand, Dave pumped Jason's hand enthusiastically. 'Thank you, Flight Sergeant.' Breaking off the clasp, the Scout Leader gave the Scouts salute.

Jason gave a brisk military salute back. 'I wish you safety. Remember that address you must visit?'

Dave patted his pocket, nodding, raising himself to his saddle, placing one foot on a pedal and shouting, 'Troop, move out.'

As a line of Scouts, two-abreast, moved off ahead of him, Dave placed his other foot on a pedal and wobbled off, the bicycle twisting to each side. After a few metres, he rode in a confident, straight line.

Jason watched them go, riding towards their Scout hut, freewheeling down the steep hill before banking left and disappearing, two by two. Sensing Imo drawing up beside him, he wished aloud, 'I hope these back roads won't have much activity.'

'I made Hazel repeat the route to me until she was memory perfect. She's got her map, too. With Austin by her side, he'll keep her correct.'

Laughing, 'Just like I keep you correct.'

'Ha!' she shouted down the empty High Street. 'You wish, Cowboy!'

Unwrapping a chocolate bar, snapping it in two, he handed her a half. 'Best we walk to the Land Rover and get to our next destination.' He tapped his earpiece, now firmly in place, and pointed to her dangling one. 'Pop it in. The colonel says there are eight heat signatures coming from Crathes Castle. Judging by their movements over the last few days, he thinks they are uninfected, hiding out.'

'Or the ghosts!'

Staring at her blood-streaked face, 'I think any castle ghost would be more afraid of you!'

Slapping his shoulder, 'Cheeky fucker.' Grinning, and throwing a treat for Sabre, she was glad it was just the three of them again.

Chapter 27

Cranking the gears, swearing at the gearstick, Imo ploughed through the pile of bodies that the drone missile had decimated. Bumping onto the pavement, she edged their way around the deep crater. The Land Rover swayed as she bumped over debris and crushed limbless torsos. Skidding to the left, the vehicle splashed through the puddles of blood and entrails.

Trees above had rows of rooks and ravens sitting patiently on thick branches. Their beaks were stained red. They were preparing to fly back down for their free feed the Hellfire had provided, like food from the Gods.

Sabre circled around in the back, lying, then standing. He nosed aside spent shell cases like he was toying with a snuffle mat filled with food.

Imo slowed and turned to her right.

'Where are you going? Crathes Castle is on the left. There's no sense in parking here. It has a long drive to the buildings.'

Pointing at a large green Pullman train with black and yellow livery. Attached to it were three long mustard and brown carriages with a dull red lower border. Imo grinned.

'It's a steam train. I'm not turning down the chance to step aboard.'

Laughing, Jason winked at her. 'What is it with you and trains?'

Driving past the sign which displayed, 'Milton of Crathes', Imo swerved to the right. She drew alongside the smaller sign with an arrow which pointed to the Royal Deeside Railway. Racing around to the tailgate, she lowered it and clucked for Sabre to join her. Together, they ran to a low white picket fence. Not bothering to open its gate, they jumped over it and ran up a ramp to a waiting room.

Jason, sighing, jumped onto the back of the Land Rover and rummaged in the kit-bags. Shaking his head as he went from one to the other, he spoke into his comms. 'How about an ammo drop off?'

There was silence for a few minutes. Jason slotted a fresh combat knife into his webbing belt, taking out the last one to hand to Imo after she'd had her fun with Sabre. Picking up a brass knuckleduster, he tried it for size, couldn't get his fingers through the rings, and pocketed it for Imo.

'No can do. Helicopter is trailing the Scouts. For protection. Load up the Crathes Castle survivors and make your way to the fence.'

Swearing under his breath, Jason replied, 'Acknowledged. On our way.'

Walking up to join her, he spotted a shadow move across the windows of the second carriage. 'Probably just the sun. HQ cleared this area.' Glancing away, he watched as Imo was encouraging Sabre to join her in the open-air driver's cab. She was stood by the mighty water boiler enticing him in with a dog treat.

Sabre stood his ground, hackles raised, growling.

Laughing at their antics, Jason strode up to them, taking his time to go through the gate, glimpsing back to the carriages as he approached the dog. Tickling its ear. 'What's up, boy?'

Stooping to feed him a treat, Jason failed to see the heavy boiler door behind Imo prise open. The dog's barking disguising the metallic creak as rusty hinges protested.

A wrinkled hand was thrust out and a man in a navy boilersuit type, two-piece uniform, thick with coal dust coagulated with blood, pushed himself out.

'C'mon Sabre, there's nothing to be frightened of,' encouraged Imo. Patting her thighs, she tempted him on with soothing noises.

The cotton drill overall-wearing man's teeth were bared, thick saliva drooling down, running from his chin to the footplate. Swiftly reaching forward, wrapping his arm around Imo. His thick limb squeezing her neck, drowning out her cry of surprise. Drawing her back, causing her heels to thump on the floor as she dug her feet in, then scrabbled for footing.

Sabre ran forward, fear of the locomotive gone. He jumped across the gap between the platform and the cab, landing a foot away from his mistress.

Turning, Jason let off an expletive as he saw the grotesque dance Imo was performing with her infected partner. Reaching for his Glock, he mouthed another swear word as he recalled he had no more ammunition, nor a gun. Drawing his combat knife, he ran towards the cab.

The dog ran from side to side, teeth snarling and gnashing in vain. He could not get to his mistress.

Imo's hands danced around, trying to get a hold of her attacker. She finally found purchase on the floor and used this to thrust back, forcing her attacker to hit his flank on the open door of the giant kettle, the open boiler.

Winded, the man released his grip and Imo seized the nearby coal shovel with both hands, twisted and brought it down on the man's head.

Dazed, he fell backwards and received another whack to the head, full on the face. He slunk to the floor.

Raising the coal shovel high in the air, twisting it at an angle, Imo screamed hoarsely as she buried it, edge first, between the bridge of his nose and eyes. As she forced it down, she heard cartilage and bone snap and felt a warm flow of blood pour over the handle and onto her fingers. Two eyeballs popped out, trailing their optic nerves. Relinquishing her hold, she unknotted the red neckerchief from around his neck and wiped her fingers clean.

Mouth agape, Jason stopped worrying about their armaments running dry. Imo was their most lethal weapon, he thought.

Doubled over, Imo gave a few gasping breaths. 'Where the hell did he come from? I thought the drone had checked this area for heat signatures.'

Pointing to the large cylindrical front of the steam train's engine, Jason shrugged. 'I guess if he was hiding in there during the flypast, the material encasing the boiler may have hidden his heat signature. I don't know. Maybe lead or asbestos?'

Looking down at the corpse, Imo glibly exclaimed, 'I dig trains, man!'

Chapter 28

Strolling down the platform, Imo led them to the waiting room. It was a Victorian style replica, which would have had a section devoted for males and another for females. This one had a sizeable area so that families could be together as they rode the short, reconstructed line and enjoyed an ice cream from the small shop. The dull mustard external woodwork of the single storey building matched that of the adjacent carriage's paint. It looked like the decorator lacked imagination or had ordered too many tins, then mixed them with black. The slate roof ran down a slope with no chance of giving purchase to any hiding infected. Its chimney pot looked like it had come from someone's garden and should have flowers growing from it.

'I'll have a look in. My uncle loved trains. This line wasn't up and running when he was alive. I've never been.'

Jason handed her a knife, waited for her to pull the sheath through her belt, then gave her the brass knuckleduster.

'Cool!' she declared, sliding it effortlessly through her fingers, closing her hand around it. She gave the air several punches. Keeping it on, she entered the room.

Sabre followed her through with no hesitation, his hackles were gone. Sniffing the air, he gave a snort and also entered the room.

Holding her nose, Imo wandered over to a hatchway, swotting at flies feasting on rows of colours in tubs. Thick, congealed cream floated in rank water. A round metal scoop lay next to brittle cone wafers. 'Oh, man, I'd love an ice cream.' Tutting, she walked around the wood-panelled room. She pushed at the ancient stove's chimney and squinted at black and white photos of trains and carriages. Pulling at one she'd studied longer than the rest; she cursed as she found it screwed to the wall.

Jason thrust out a Leatherman, a tool he'd found during the second inspection of the kit-bags. 'We've one each. Keep it. Fold it out and it has a screwdriver. Are you expecting to get home soon so you can display it on your wall?' Squinting at her, 'I don't even know where you live.'

'Nowhere special,' she replied absently. 'Prison keeps me with a roof over my head. And well-fed. I've not had a home of my own since the council made me give up the tenancy when my aunt died. They wouldn't let me transfer it. Said I had to go onto the bottom of the list. Got a spell in prison over it.'

Jason raised an eyebrow.

'Well. The smug shit at the Council office was asking for it.' Looking at him with a grin, 'I only punched him the once.' Whistling, she unscrewed the photo and carefully took down the frame.

'You can keep it with your cash and jewellery.'

'Ah.' Looking down at her feet, 'You found them.'

'Enough to start your own branch of Ramsdens!' quipped Jason.

'Just saving for my retirement. Not everyone has a military pension.'

Smiling, Jason wondered if they had restarted his. Each week soon built up. 'I doubt I'd be able to access the paymaster. Seen enough?'

'Yeah, it's an accurate reproduction of a Victorian waiting room. This would have been a great local attraction.' Sighing, 'My uncle would have loved it.' Thrusting the painting into Jason's hands, careful of her knuckleduster, 'Here, hold this. I'll spend a penny while I'm here. I bet they've the old-fashioned porcelain toilets.' She gave a playful wince. 'Cold on the bum, though.'

Walking off with Sabre in tow, she held the door open for the dog, looking at Jason and tutting. 'I would appreciate a bit of privacy from you.'

Rolling his eyes, Jason walked out of the waiting room and sauntered over to the carriages. Peering in, he marvelled at the plump floral cushions of the upright seats with railway logo embroidered headrests. The wooden tables shone with lacquer. His head snapped up as the door at the end of the carriage cracked open and a woman with a shiny peaked cap, black waistcoat and tartan skirt jumped down. She ran, head down, towards Jason, roaring.

Jumping back, Jason swung the picture, bashing it against her intended headbutt. Her head tore through the picture, the glass severing her carotid artery. She faltered, crashing into a Victorian lamppost, dropping to the ground, shattering the wooden frame as she fell. Blood sprayed out, bringing thick speckles of colour to the grey concrete.

'My fucking picture!' screamed Imo, joining them. 'That would have looked lovely on my wall.'

'Your prison wall?' He leaned forward and puked over the white picket fence into some bushes.

'For my new flat. I've saved enough for a deposit.'

'You mean you've stolen enough?'

'Get stuffed! I've earned that money.'

Looking at the dead woman and then at Imo's blood-stained fatigues, 'You have. Sorry. I doubt anyone is keeping count.'

'Knowing my luck, they will be. I'm just taking it day by day.' She patted her nearest pouch and whispered, 'I keep the most valuable jewellery and cash in here. Whoever replenishes our Land Rover won't be stealing this.'

He gave her a conspiratorial wink. 'Shall we go?'

Running off with Sabre, she pointed to the bushes. 'I spotted some wild brambles. We'll go out the gate and follow the nature trail path and have a scoff. Want some?'

She was out of earshot when he replied, 'Not for me. I find them too sweet. They leave me feeling sick.'

Chapter 29

Imo, wiping at her purple, sticky mouth, belched. 'I don't remember brambles being this strange tasting. Sabre wouldn't eat his.'

Jason looked to his left and smirked.

'I don't know why you bother looking for traffic,' teased Imo. 'We are the only people daft enough to be driving.' She crossed to the open, tall, black gates with the inevitable spikes. They drove past the East Lodge. This low, grey bricked house had white crisscross windows that wouldn't have looked out of place in a Norman church. The Land Rover approached the long drive, cruising parallel with what looked like a man-made small lake. A digger laid abandoned by a mound of earth. Imo skidded their vehicle to a halt. A thick tree laid across the road, its branches spread out on the grass to their right, earthen roots to their left. More stuck in the air, their leaves rotting. Trees were unevenly spread on either side of the road, stretching upwards towards the castle.

Leaning forward, Jason uttered, 'Someone has deliberately cut that. Probably with a chainsaw. Look at the nice clean line.'

'No way around it, too many trees.' Fingering her catapult through the fabric of her thigh pocket, 'Bet there are lots of squirrels.'

'Find a way round,' barked the colonel in their earpieces.

'The fucker has cameras everywhere. I think he's the new creep in our lives!'

'I'm the old creepy fucker. Now get to the castle!'

'All right, Robin Hood, we'll rescue Maid Marian in our own time,' jested Imo, staring at the fallen tree.

Opening his door, Jason strode around to the back of the Land Rover, hefting off a kit-bag containing food and drink. 'I'll carry this. They are bound to be hungry.'

'Assuming they've got the intelligence correct this time.' She peered into the distance. 'How far?'

'Probably one mile.'

'Fuck that!' she exclaimed, looking at the kit-bag and slamming the Land Rover into reverse. 'Jump back on. I have an idea!'

Imo kicked the huge black tyre. 'The lentil brigade failed to deflate this bad boy. Hazel kept the seats warm.' With a twinkle in her eye, she asked, 'What do you think?'

Jason looked up at the monster truck. 'It's perfect. If only we had the key.'

'Ta da!' She dangled a keyring in front of his eyes. A solitary car key jingling against the metal.

'How on earth do you have it?'

'I spotted Hazel throwing it away. I wasn't going to pass the opportunity to drive this bad boy.'

'You are brilliant. Eight souls, hopefully uninfected, owe their lives to you.'

She curtsied. 'You're welcome!'

'Get settled in the cab and I'll pass the kit-bags. Then I'll drive us there.'

'Fuck that,' she grinned. 'I'll drive. I've dreamt of this since seeing them in the show in Aberdeen years ago.'

'Working the show?'

'Of course,' she replied slyly, mimicking picking his pocket.

'You're an education!'

Beaming, she clambered up the ladder to the cabin and thrust out a hand for the first kit-bag. Puffing, 'Rip out that advertising banner over there. The long bits of wood should take the weight of my boy. He can use it as a ramp to get in.'

Jason threw up the last kit-bag and extracted his Leatherman from his pocket, muttering, 'She thinks more about that dog than me. I would have made him run behind us.'

Imo waited patiently, all the while talking to Sabre as the dog sat under the open door.

Jason wedged the long plank of wood into the grass and tilted the other end to the open door of the monster truck. He pushed at the wood, about a third of the way up. It wobbled. 'I doubt it'll take his weight. His claws won't have much to hold on. It's too smooth.'

'Stop fretting. Give his flank a push up.' She stuck her index finger in the air. 'Careful not to get your finger in his arse! My boy is too young for a prostate exam!'

Holding the wood, Jason stuck his tongue out at her. He shuffled aside and coaxed the dog. 'Up you go, Sabre. Get to your mummy.'

Sabre whimpered and took a few steps back, looking like he was dancing and preparing for a talent show performance.

'Up you come, boy,' shouted Imo, holding her arms out.

The dog gave a bark, ran at the wood, scurried halfway up, and slid.

Jason pushed the dog up, straining at his weight. 'A bit of help!' he yelled breathlessly.

Imo dangled out of the door, looking like she was going headfirst down a leisure pool slide. Reaching, she grabbed Sabre's collar and pulled. With her other hand, she grabbed him by the scruff of his neck and yanked him aboard. She ignored his high-pitched yelp, like a vet had come behind him, and clamped his testicles.

A bushy tail was tucked in, the wood was thrust aside, and the door slammed shut. A roaring engine coughed into life and the monster truck drove down the park, trailing chunks of ploughed up earth like a weaving tractor. The mighty car stopped; the passenger door was pushed open. 'Keep up, Cowboy. You can trot along, like a faithful hound.'

'You heard?'

'Yes, you ungrateful sod. Sabre is part of our team. He's saved both of our lives.' She revved the engine and drove another few metres. The metal ladder was tossed down. 'Climb up, don't forget to bring the ladder. I don't want you breaking a leg when you need to exit.'

Stepping into the cabin, he pushed against Sabre to encourage him in the back seats. The dog remained firmly sat, tongue lolloping, panting away, looking out the windscreen.

'In the back, Cowboy, my boy is riding shotgun.'

Jason, muttering under his breath, climbed through the back, carefully dragging the small metal ladder.

Pointing to a pile of sleeping bags and blankets, Imo laughed, 'You've made your bed, now you can lie in it.'

Chapter 30

Leaning over the headrests, staring at the fallen tree as Imo idled the engine, Jason advised, 'Take it slowly.'

Throwing the gear into reverse, 'Fuck that. I want some fun. Hang on, Sabre.' She moved the vehicle ten metres away, revved, then floored the accelerator. The monster truck hit the oak tree at speed. Thick wheels dug into the bark, splintering, then shattering it as they rose, seemed to falter in mid-air, then went crashing down on the other side. The rear wheels followed faithfully, repeating the performance.

Sabre bumped against the door, then the windscreen, yelping as the movements threw him back onto his seat.

Jason cursed Imo as his head bashed against the front headrests, then knocked on the cabin roof. He braced himself against Sabre's seat as he felt the rear wheels catch in protest against the wood, struggle and then gain a hold.

Imo let off a rebel yell, like a Confederate soldier in the American Civil War. Clutching the steering wheel, she maintained her balance as the tree trunk shattered in two. Like a ship's mast breaking in a storm. Driving up the road, she ignored the signs advising her that twenty was plenty and gunned the engine.

Jason jumped back into his seat, wrestling with the seatbelt which was caught up on the ladder's rungs. He gave up as Imo drew to a halt by rows of timber and glass greenhouses. 'Drive right up to the castle. We can fit the eight survivors in the cabin. It'll be a tight squeeze, but they'll be safe from roaming infected.'

'Look ahead,' hissed Imo.

Squinting through the windscreen, Jason thought he was seeing double. Two women, side by side, blocking the road. Each had a serene look on their long faces. Mousy hair curled around their shoulders. They were each wearing a mauve dress flowing to their ankles. Open-toed sandals adorned their bare feet. They both carried a low wicker basket brimming with tomatoes and strawberries. They could have been twins, except one looked ten years younger and didn't have the telltale crow's feet around her eyes that her companion had.

'How on earth have they survived?' marvelled Jason.

'Strawberries look good. I hope they taste better than those brambles.' Imo pointed to a low wall to her left, waited for the women to move, and parked the truck. Careful to pocket the keys, she slid along to sit by Sabre, opened the door and jumped onto the wall. Clucking, she encouraged Sabre to do the same and watched him carefully, ensuring he didn't fall. She left the door open and heard a shout from the cabin, 'Still sulking?'

'Welcome, sister,' greeted the younger woman. 'Have you come to follow Him?'

Springing from the wall, Sabre following, Imo looked around. 'Who?'

'The enlightened one,' beamed the older woman.

Turning when she heard Jason stumble onto the wall and jump from it, she whispered, 'Welcome to the funny farm!'

Raising her basket, revealing her slender arm as her sleeve rode up, the woman on the left smiled. 'Join us in our daily feast. We have gathered His lunch. God has smiled down upon us and given us the bounty of his land.'

'That's nice!' beamed Imo. 'We've a few boxes of rations we can contribute. Spam fritters all round.'

'Oh no!' hissed the older woman. 'All animals are God's creatures. Processed food is a thing of the past. The scourge has provided a time of cleansing. Please leave your rations behind and prepare for your new life. Your man can come too, but will have to earn his keep.'

Imo turned to Jason, beaming. 'Come, man, join me.'

The two women turned as one, carrying their harvest past a large car park and several old buildings. Veering to the left, they strode down a small but steep hill and entered a ground floor door.

Staring up, Jason marvelled at the turreted castle. Its National Trust for Scotland flag cracked in the wind, the high flagpole swaying like a first-time cruise ship passenger. He counted six floors to this tower house and a battlement type roof with soaring chimneys. This was a family home made to look like a defensible castle. Feeling nude without his pistol and rifle, Jason fingered his combat knife as he looked nervously around.

'Do not worry. He has protected us from the scourge victims. You are safe with us,' reassured the older woman, leading Jason by the hand. She gently took him into a cavernous kitchen. His boots echoing on the concrete flooring and resounding against the clinically white tiles. Brass pots of varying sizes were lined in a row on a shelf, beneath them, on another shelf, herbs were drying.

The other woman followed them in, beckoning for Imo to join them. Tapping the door lintel, 'Mind your head.'

They placed two baskets on the tall, wide kitchen table that looked like it was made from one tree trunk. A damp patch gave away that someone had scrubbed it clean.

The sweet, yeasty smell of fresh bread filled the room.

Jason's belly rumbled. Sniffing deeply, 'Any chance of a sandwich? I haven't had fresh bread for weeks. It smells delicious.' He looked from stranger to stranger with a hopeful smile.

A woman wearing the same mauve dress as the others walked in. She wore a garland of flowers around her head, like a floral crown, holding her long hair in place. Her piercing blue eyes squinted at Jason, her nose wrinkled when she saw his blood-stained clothing and muddy boots. 'I heard we had guests. You must change into a robe before being presented to Him.'

Laughing, Imo suggested, 'He'll be a size twelve dress.'

Turning, looking Imo up and down, tutting, with a deep frown, the woman scowled, 'As will you, young woman. He will be most interested in you.'

Smirking, Jason whispered, 'Dazzle Him with your teeth!'

'Fuck off!' she retorted.

A collective gasp escaped from the three women's lips.

'Look, we are here to take you all to safety. Could you please gather the other five and we'll be on our way?' requested Jason.

'But this is our place of safety,' reasoned the new woman. Tilting her head, ignoring the daisy that fell off, she emphasised, 'With Him.'

'Bring the fella too,' mocked Imo. 'The more the merrier. Out of interest, how did you survive the -' hesitating, she continued with, 'the scourge?'

The younger of the women smiled. 'We were the chosen ones.'

Slapping her palm against her forehead, Imo retorted with, 'Of course you were.'

'We witnessed the death of the sinners all around us, as they ate other sinners. Our souls were pure, and we gathered here. The white smoke drew us to Him. He fed us and has been nourishing us since,' claimed the garland wearing woman.

Walking up to her, then to the other two women, Imo gave each a smile, glancing into their eyes. Returning to Jason, talking a plate from him that he'd been given by the younger woman, Imo hissed, 'Best not eat or drink anything. They are high on something. Eyes are pinpoints. He's drugged them. Creepy fucker.'

Frowning, Jason looked longingly at his tomato and basil sandwich. 'Oh, man. Fresh bread as well.'

Imo threw him an oats and honey crunch bar from her pouch and dropped a dog biscuit for Sabre.

'The dog will have to go outside,' the older woman ordered. 'It is unclean. He insists on cleanliness.'

'Sounds like a controlling fucker,' hissed Imo. Louder, she insisted, 'Sabre goes where I go.'

Three more gasps broke out. The younger one exclaimed, 'Please. No more foul language, and certainly not in His presence. The animal must go outside.'

The far-off door opened. A slim, edging on gaunt, bearded man strutted in. He wore a simple white robe, stretching from his neck to his ankles. It was tightened around his waist with a tartan tasselled cord, looking like it belonged to a dressing-gown. Long hair flowed down his back, tied neatly in a tight ponytail that stretched back his face. His plaited hair bounced as he strode towards Jason, Imo, and Sabre.

'And who the fuck are you?' challenged Imo.

'I'm Adam.'

Chapter 31

'Of course you are,' laughed Imo. Pointing to the older woman, 'And I guess she's Eve. Eaten any apples lately?'

The older woman nodded. 'We are all Eve. And the orchards are bountiful.'

'It's a new birth here,' continued the man, smiling, showing off his perfect teeth. 'Our old world has gone. The scourge has refreshed it. Given us a chance to begin again. Our Eden provides us with a bountiful supply.' He drew near to the younger woman and placed his palm on her stomach. 'And one day we will have new growth. A chance to live without sin. I will ensure things are done correctly this time. My Father's wishes will come true.'

'And who is daddy?' asked Imo, returning the smile.

Taking a step back at the sight of her blackened teeth and stumps, Adam answered, 'Why, God, of course.'

Turning to Jason, whispering, 'He's off his meds! Thinks he's Jesus. Or that he's just been created by God. He's a fuckwit, either way.'

Nodding, Jason shook his head when Adam picked up the plate of sandwiches and thrust it under his nose.

'Oh, but you must eat,' insisted Adam. 'Afterwards, you'll be welcomed into my community. You can chop the wood, tend to the gardens, grow our crops in the walled garden and greenhouses. We can survive and flourish forever. There is also an established apiary. Honey will sustain us. Just like it sustained John the Baptist in the wilderness.'

Pushing the plate away, Jason insisted. 'Gather everyone. We need to leave in the hour. I want to move out during daylight. We've a mission to complete.'

Shaking his head vigorously, Adam insisted, 'There is no need to leave. This is our Eden. We will regrow. We will do my Father's work. But first, the dog must go outside. My temple must be kept clean.' Walking to Sabre, he grabbed the fur by his neck and immediately withdrew his hand when Sabre growled, baring his teeth.

'Not that crazy,' grinned Imo. 'Well done, boy.'

Adam strode to the door, opening it wide, pointing outside. 'The dog.' He stood with the other hand on his hip.

Imo felt in her pocket with her right hand and fumbled about, slipping her fingers through her knuckleduster. 'I'm going to enjoy knocking some sense into this stupid bugger.' She drew her hand out.

Jason, seeing the brass object around her fist, gently placed his hand on hers. 'Best not. He's obviously ill. Let the colonel deal with his crimes against these vulnerable women. Besides, they've obviously got some sort of immunity against the Russian chemicals. The boffins might learn something. They survived the attack, unmasked. We need to get them to the fence, somehow. The scientists could even find a cure by studying them.' Sighing, 'I'm tired of all the killing.'

Rolling her eyes, she turned to Adam. 'The dog stays.'

Open-mouthed, head askance, the man smoothed down his white robe. He was about to speak but was pushed to the floor as an infected man flew into the room, wrapping his arms around Adam's chest. Gripping hard, squeezing down. A shriek escaped from Adam as he fell against the Aga, knocking down a pan of water. The boiling liquid burned through the man's ragged clothing, his legs bubbling red. Adam scrambled free, running to the women, cowering behind them. He pushed two forward a foot, towards the stranger. All four squatted, hands clasped together, each mouthing a prayer in unison.

Imo ran towards the man, raining blow after blow on his face, knocking his skull against the hard metal of the Aga. His blood flowed over the tiled floor, pooling in the grouting and running down to a drain. It gurgled as loudly as the man did when Imo directed fresh blows to his windpipe, forcing it back through his neck, deviating it. A sharp crack signalling the end of the attacker.

Jason picked the man up by his shoulders, dragging him to the door, manhandling him outside. Slamming the door closed, he locked it, first with the key, then ramming home the top and bottom bolts. 'There may be others. Where is the main entrance?'

Stammering, Adam pointed through the door. 'Up one flight. Take the door on the narrow landing. That's the only other way into the castle.'

Running, Jason took the stone steps two at a time, Sabre running after him. He dived through a thick wooden door, its ancient metalwork creaking at the intrusion. Entering a large room, he spied the window and the double door to its left. Sprinting to it, he slammed home a wooden beam that secured both halves of the door together, then turned the large key. Pulling the doorknob, he nodded in satisfaction that he'd secured the building.

Footsteps echoed from the stairwell, and a lithe woman entered. Her black skin shone in the well-lit vestibule. She'd rolled the sleeves of her mauve dress up, revealing short tufts of hair in her armpit. Her skin was covered in purple and dark yellow bruises of varying shades. Each were rounded with a tiny bullseye in the centre. She pointed accusingly at him. 'Friend, who are you? Turn and show me your eyes.'

Jason smiled. 'Nice to meet you. What's your name?'

Her brown lips, tinged with a red streak, lifted. 'Eve. We thought He was the only male survivor.' Looking Jason up and down, her thick lips opening as she beamed.

'Got yourself a date?' snapped Imo as she pushed the woman aside. Stepping in from what was the servant's staircase, Imo frowned at Jason. 'The shotgun and those precious five cartridges are back in the Land Rover. Someone thought food to be more important. Look outside.'

Jason peered through the narrow slitted window. 'Ah. The colonel's intelligence is wrong today.'

'Never trust a man in uniform,' muttered Imo, heading up a short flight of stairs. Holding up a bloodied hand wrapped around her knuckleduster, 'All I've got is this and a knife. Oh, and the screwdriver. I could use the scissors attachment to cut the infected to death.' Sarcastically, she continued, 'If they'd politely wait until I work out how to use the Leatherman.'

'There are three more of them,' observed Jason.

'No shit, Sherlock,' retorted Imo as she entered a room with enormous windows along one wall. She discounted the view across a well-manicured lawn. Imo scanned the room, spotting the yellow sofas and matching lamps on the mahogany tables. Her boots thumped on the solid wood flooring near the large red rug. Ignoring the disapproving looks glaring down from the oil painted men on the walls, she returned to Jason and pointed up. 'Stoop over, I'll jump on your back and reach for them.'

Grinning at her intended prize, he snapped, 'No way. Not with those boots on.' Dragging a chest of drawers over, he swiped away some ornaments and a vase, not caring they were priceless antiques. They shattered on the stone floor as he jumped onto the historic furniture and reached up and unhooked a long spear. Holding the sharp point in the air, he passed the brass and wooden handle end to Imo.

Her eyes lit up as she tested the pointed end, larger than her hand, the metalwork stretching further than her wrist.

Jason offered a wooden shield to Eve, who shook her head, mouth agape. 'This is His temple. How dare you?'

'Fuck this!' Imo strode over to her, taking off her knuckleduster, and punched her on the bridge of her nose.

Eve dropped, blood gushing from her nose. Imo opened several drawers, found a cloth, bunched it up and pushed it against Eve's nose. She turned the unconscious woman over, so her body weight pushed against the cloth, stemming the flow of blood. Looking up, Imo shouted, 'What? It's one way of getting them into the truck. I'm not hanging around without decent weapons, while the infected grow in numbers.'

Holding up a spear and a shield, Jason shook his head disapprovingly.

'Ha! Forget Adam and his Eves.' Pointing to his chest, 'You Tarzan, me Jane!'

Chapter 32

Sprinting up to the larger room above, Imo tore at the thick curtains, pulling free their cords from each side. Saluting clumsily at the nearest portrait, 'Sorry, your Lordship!' Returning to the unconscious Eve, she pulled out her Leatherman. Fumbling with its attachments, she locked the blade and sliced neatly through the cord. 'Cool. I'll keep this tool.' She turned Eve onto her stomach, twisted her hands behind her back and tied them, doing the same with her feet. Turning to Jason, as he entered the room, 'I'm glad the pervert likes his women thin; I reckon you can carry her to the truck.'

'And what will you be doing?'

Grinning, Imo glanced at Sabre. 'My boy and I have work to do!' Beating the spear against her shield, she sounded like an inept drummer in a teenage band. Walking to the stairwell, she shouted back at him, 'Bring her along. We might persuade Adam to give a hand. He likes his women submissive.'

Rolling his eyes, straining at his knees, Jason hoisted the woman over one shoulder, grabbing a spear with the other hand. He grunted as he followed her, Sabre's tail swishing between them, the dog's bum wiggling as he carefully stepped down each stair, paws splayed.

A high-pitched scream welcomed them into the kitchen. The four Eves were gathered around Adam, stroking his hair, cheeks, and arms. Together they were murmuring in low voices, repeating a collective prayer. Their eyes were closed. Adam's weren't. He was too busy screaming rather than praying. 'What have you done to Wednesday Eve?'

Jason narrowing his eyes, cocking his head. Then a grin. 'One for everyday of the week. Seven women and you. Lucky boy!' He swiped away the plate of sandwiches on the long table and carefully placed Wednesday Eve on it, putting her in the recovery position as best as he could. 'Or naughty boy?' Checking her airway, he placed the cloth under her nose again.

'Or a fucking pervert? Praying on these vulnerable women,' snarled Imo.

A smirk quickly appeared on Adam's face, then was wiped clear immediately. He placed his hands on each of the bowed women's heads, winking at Imo. 'Join us. You could be my spare Eve, for when the other's monthlies visit.'

'Get to fuck!' shouted Imo, raising her spear.

Leaving Wednesday Eve, Jason strode between them, turning to Imo, whispering, 'Remember, we need them alive.'

Walking to the door, 'Let's clear the area, and get the tied-up woman into the back of the truck.'

Nodding, Sabre sat beside him, Jason counted down from three to one.

Imo unlocked and unbolted the door, thrust it open and ran outside, spear held at right angles. The wide blade burst through the mauve dress of a surprised woman. Streaks of grey in her mousy hair, wrinkled skin that hung in bags around her eyes, which were wide in pain as she looked down, grappling at the shaft of the spear. Gasping as bright red blood poured from her mouth, she fell forward. Letting go of the spear, Imo watched as the woman, another Eve, impaled herself further when her weight dropped onto the spear, wedged in the path. The blade exited her back like she was being skewered for a barbeque. 'Oops!' exclaimed Imo.

'Jesus! Not another innocent killed,' blurted Jason, dropping his spear. Walking to the woman, he cradled her lifeless face. 'You poor soul.' Turning to Imo, seeing her look at her feet. 'We'll take her corpse. The scientists can perform a post-mortem and learn from her body.'

Imo wrestled the woman to the ground, the pole sticking proudly in the air. Standing on her chest, foot cracking ribs and burying itself in her chest, Imo pulled and grunted. 'Er. How are we going to remove her skewer? She'll never fit in the truck like this.' She waved Sabre away from the woman's corpse.

Gagging, running to the nearest bush, Jason vomited, wiped his mouth, and returned to Imo. He didn't look at the body as Imo tugged her foot free and shook it.

Biting his lip, Jason studied the woman for several seconds. 'Change of plan. Leave her and we'll let the colonel know her location. If the scientists want her, they can come for her rotting corpse.'

'I already know,' a deep voice growled down their comms.

Imo glanced at the walls, spotted the camera, and waved. Pointing at the corpse, she then gave the CCTV camera a thumbs up and a wink.

'Yes, yes, well done. Good kill. Shame it was a friendly. Now look behind you, Poacher,' warned the colonel.

A man in a bulky white suit, protective face netting covering his head, wobbling with each stride, was screaming as he came sprinting down the hill towards them. He carried a metal can, like he was pouring oil.

Banging heads in their haste to reach Jason's dropped spear, Imo recovered first, grabbing it, and advancing to the stranger. Holding her spear firmly, she gave a loud ululation that rolled around her tongue.

'I can't see through his beekeeper's veil if his eyes are red,' shouted Jason.

Imo continued running, met the man and pierced the shield through his hood, impaling him under his chin. As she felt it crunch through, she reached up and tore off his hood and stared into his dying eyes. A red glow dimmed, turning scarlet, then a dull brown as he gasped his last. 'Well, I'll be,' she quipped, releasing her hold on the spear. Walking away, nodding to Jason.

Hand to his mouth, he suggested, 'Let's get Wednesday Eve into the truck's cabin.'

As they entered the kitchen, Imo opened several drawers and grinned when she saw the huge meat cleaver. Grabbing the handle, she gave the blade several swipes in the air, narrowly missing Adam. 'Jesus! I could have killed you.'

'Adam. Jesus came later,' corrected Jason with a wink, bolting the door behind them as Sabre's bushy tail cleared the frame.

Taking her free hand, Adam whispered to her, 'Join us. A vacancy has opened. We can mate every Thursday.'

Struggling out of his grip, pushing him away, Imo spat at him. Her saliva dripped from his white robe. 'You'll get in that truck and bring the surviving women with you. Then we are getting out of here.'

He placed both hands in front of him and clasped them together. Looking down at his disciples, who were trying in vain to loosen their bound sister's knots, he raised his voice. 'Why would I want to leave here? The women and I are re-setting the world. Each Eve will repopulate in nine months and flourish from there.' Lowering his voice, 'I have different fanny every night. What man would want to leave that?' Winking, staring at Imo's crotch, 'I bet yours is nice and tight. You'd be a feisty one.'

'Not so mental then, just a randy sod,' hissed Imo, dropping the blade. Slipping her hand in her pocket, fumbling, putting on a show for Adam. Watching his eyes light up as her fingers roamed near her genitals. A bulge protruded low down in his robe. Whipping her hand out, she flashed bronze as shiny as the pans lined against the kitchen wall. Punching Adam under the jaw, laughing as she heard metal crunch on bone.

Adam whipped backwards, knocked off his feet, landing face-first in the crack of Wednesday Eve's bottom. His nose buried itself where her thighs started and blood started soaking into her dress, turning it purple.

The other Eves flocked to him like bees to honey, turning him over, checking his broken jaw. Running their hands carefully over his body.

'It'll take more than a monthly amount of nursing to recover from that cracker!' jibed Imo, marvelling at the effects of her punch.

The younger Eve screamed and ran for Imo, neither hearing the warning shouted by Jason.

Imo struck out at the advancing head, striking at the woman's temple. Her skull shattered, bits of bone protruding from the skin, then blood poured down the surprised woman's face as she crumpled at Imo's feet.

'What the fuck, Imo,' screamed Jason. 'Alive I said.'

'It's not a problem. There are no cameras in here. Besides, she came at me. We can leave her body here for any clean-up team to investigate.' Turning to the unconscious Adam, 'Your temple is crumbling!'

Chapter 33

Striding between the surviving cowering women, Jason lowered his voice, hoping to sound sincere and reassuring. 'Please. Take Wednesday Eve to our truck, then lift Adam into it. We need to leave here and get you somewhere safe.'

'No,' hissed one of the Eve's, her eyes narrowing. 'We stay with Him.' Taking Adam's hand, rubbing furiously, trying to revive him.

'Suit yourselves. Where is the missing Eve? He said there were seven of you?'

'In her bedchamber. She is unclean,' said the older Eve.

'She is washing?'

Imo, cleaver back in hand, 'She means she's having her period. On the blob. The decorators are in. Need anymore?'

Blushing, Jason kicked Adam, ignoring the gasps from the women. 'It's like he's gone back in time. He really wanted to reset the world. What a dick.' Pushing the women's hands away, he bent down, bound Adam and heaved him onto his shoulders. 'Get the door, Imo. We'll do this ourselves. Come with me but watch our back from these and any infected.'

Giving a few furious swipes of the cleaver, Imo kept the Eves at bay, then unbolted the door and held it open while Jason struggled out with Adam.

Sabre sat by the women, growling at them.

They scrambled back, away from the dog's teeth, hunkering against the wall.

Cocking his ears, hearing a whistle, Sabre ran from them, licking at the blood on the floor as he bolted from the room.

'Aren't you worried they are going to lock the castle? They could remain in there for weeks with the food we've seen in the kitchen. They were harvesting, drying, and pickling from the greenhouses and land for weeks.'

Puffing, Jason shook his head. 'They won't want to be far from this dickhead. Besides, I have an idea.'

'Care to share it?' asked Imo as she jumped on the wall beside the truck and opened its door. Rummaging in the back, she pulled out some green paracord from a kit-bag. 'You didn't leave everything behind in the Land Rover.'

Together, they bundled Adam into the back of the cabin, tied him up, ignored his groans, and laid him on the blankets. He slipped back into unconsciousness.

'Lock the doors,' ordered Jason. 'Then watch my back.' Whistling for Sabre, he ran back to the castle.

Arriving at the door before Imo, he slipped through the open doorway, stopping in his tracks as a fifth mauve dressed woman was in the room. She was crouched by the cowering women, her brow furrowed.

Grinning as she entered, spying the newcomer, Imo chortled. 'The missing Eve.' Seeing the red stains at the front and back of her dress, 'I guess the decorators have gone.' Looking around the blood-splattered walls, 'They might have started in here!'

'Come with us, please,' beseeched Jason to the newcomer.

'Who are you? What's happening?'

'When did you last eat or drink?' asked Jason gently.

'Yesterday. Probably in the afternoon, maybe midday. Why?'

Turning to Imo, Jason nodded. 'You were right about the sandwiches and other food.' Pointing to the older woman, 'I guess you were in on it?'

Looking down, she nodded slowly. 'Adam made me. He said I wasn't much use to him now that I was menopausal. Before he'd used me, he would say I was too dry to, you know -' Pointing to her lap, she continued, 'He said he'd use my mouth instead.' Creasing her face in painful recollection, 'I was to be banished if I didn't comply with putting the powder and sometimes liquid on the food and into the drink.

Sometimes there would be injections. To keep them topped up, he would joke.' Turning to the others, 'Sorry.' She burst into tears.

The other women, except for the newcomer, wrapped her in their arms, making soothing noises. Their faces of concern showing no sign of realising what had happened to them.

The newcomer walked over to Jason. 'I don't understand what is happening. I've had no memory since taking my son to school. Please let me leave here and find him and return to my husband. Then I think I need to go to the police.' Squinting her eyes at their clothing. 'Why is the army here?'

'Air Force, ma'am,' corrected Jason, automatically. 'Follow us. We'll get you to a place of safety.' Stooping, Imo stopped him.

'Save your knees and back. I know you are getting old!' she teased. Bending, she lifted Wednesday Eve with ease while juggling her cleaver. The bound woman went over her left shoulder. Imo didn't flinch when the woman's head struck the edge of the table. Instead, she strode effortlessly out of the building.

Taking the newcomer by the hand, Jason encouraged her to walk with him. 'What's your name?' he asked as she took a few tentative steps to the doorway.

Frowning, she stopped. 'I don't know.' Stammering in reply, 'Everything is fuzzy.'

'Just keep walking. You are doing so well.' Looking back as they exited the building, he smiled in satisfaction to see the Eves rising to their feet, all heads turning in his direction.

Reaching the truck, Jason jumped onto the low wall, holding out his hand for her to do the same. Clasping hers, he helped her into the cabin.

Shrieking as she climbed in, she pointed to Wednesday Eve and then Adam. 'Those eyes!' Crinkling her nose when she saw the dried blood around his lower face. 'He,' she began. 'He,' her voice faltered.

Placing his hand on her left shoulder, Jason gently twisted her round and guided her into the passenger seat. 'Best you look forward. He's tied up and will get what's coming to him when we get you to safety. We've a drive ahead of us. Close your eyes and rest. He's gone back to sleep. He'll not be waking up for a few hours.' Whistling, then pointing at the generous footwell. 'Our dog is a big softy. He'll fit in there. Just mind your feet.'

A fluffy black and tan shape leapt onto the driver's seat, then dived into the adjacent footwell when Jason threw a dog treat.

Imo squashed into the driver's seat, pushing Jason to the left with her hip. 'I'm driving,' she claimed.

Looking at the tearful woman, he shook his head. 'I'll take a turn. We need a bit of care now.'

Cursing, wriggling around Jason, Imo winked at the woman. 'Budge up, there's room for two.' As she coaxed some room, she leant forward and made a fuss of Sabre. 'What's the plan, Cowboy?'

Jason turned the engine over and drove slowly away, eyes constantly in the truck's mirrors. He smiled when he saw the mauve-dressed figures walk, then run after him. 'You know in the television programmes when a character finds someone who's taken a drug overdose and is semi-conscious? They get them walking around the room, slapping their face to keep them awake, while waiting for an ambulance?'

Imo rolled her eyes. 'Complete bollocks that.'

'Maybe. But this exercise and some time away from food and drink,' he left the sentence uncompleted for her to finish.

'Ah!' Leaning forward and to her left, squashing the other woman, Imo glanced in the mirror. 'I get you.'

'Keep driving,' ordered the colonel, interrupting them. He continued in their earpieces. 'There are two life signs in the nearby garden centre. I'll direct you. Head back into Banchory.'

Imo looked out of the windscreen, angling her head.

'Our drones have done a fresh sweep.'

'Hope they are accurate this time or someone is for the chop,' growled Imo, raising her cleaver, ignoring the whimper from the woman sharing her seat.

Laughter broke over the comms. 'I'd love you in my squadron. You are such a fighter. The ultimate killing machine.'

Covering her comms mic. 'You'll find out one day, dickhead,' snarled Imo, phlegm flying from her mouth and hitting the dashboard.

Indicating right for the benefit of the wheezing women chasing him, Jason eased the truck back onto the main road. He drove slowly past the Royal Deeside Railway, like they were tourists seeking somewhere to visit. He pulled up short of the crater in the road, waiting for their followers to catch up. When they reached the back wheels, he drove off, going wide of the crater, praying they wouldn't fall in. Crawling towards Banchory, he let out a sigh and thrust his head back onto the headrest. Staring at the far-off trees, he imagined them covered in snow, looking like a winter wonderland. His thoughts were turning to Pippa and her love for Christmas when an arm shot across from his left.

'That house!' shouted the woman, pointing to their right. Up a steep bank, behind some railings and a lawn strewn with a scooter, slide, and swing, stood a detached Victorian-era house with wide windows and a slate roof. The decaying body of a small child draped from a low stone wall that bordered a rockery. 'I know it. I think that's where I live.'

Reaching over, Imo covered the woman's eyes. 'Keep your memories. Try to remember the happy times.'

Putting his foot on the accelerator, Jason sped past the house, then slowed back to a crawl.

'Take the next right, drive up the hill, forget about the houses and the school entrance. Follow the road, it'll twist round. You can't miss the garden centre. It's well signposted,' commanded the colonel.

'I'll be there soon. I want to keep an eye on the runners. Are there any other life signs that might attack us?'

'Just the two in the garden centre. We think they are uninfected.'

Imo tutted. 'Like we can trust army intelligence.' Fingering her cleaver, 'I put my trust in weapons.' Nudging Jason in the ribs, 'Like my shotgun and cartridges.'

Ignoring her, wishing for the same, feeling vulnerable without modern fighting weapons, Jason looked down at her empty holster. Like him, she'd given her weapon away. His went to the Scout Leader, though Austin had held his hand out for it.

'Sir. We'll need re-arming when we get these civilians to safety.'

'Acknowledged,' came the curt reply.

Glancing at Imo, fighting back his tears, 'And I want time off. To visit my wife in Dundee.'

'Denied,' came the immediate reply.

'Cun-' began Imo's retort as the brakes were slammed. The trio were pushed forward, and Sabre whimpered in the footrest.

Jason, taking his hands off the steering wheel, wiped furiously at his eyes. Croaking, 'Sorry. I can't see to drive safely. I'll be fine in a minute. The women can catch up.'

Placing a hand on his, Imo leaned over to see into the mirror. 'They aren't running together. Though the old bird is holding her own. They still look eager to tear you apart, though.'

Pushing down gently on the accelerator, Jason followed the immaculate lawn and neatly manicured low bushes and entered the car park of the garden centre. Ignoring the spaces and rows of abandoned vehicles, he chided himself for not coming here for cars for the Scouts. Pulling up at the paved main doors besides two giant grey planters, one on either side of the entrance, he turned off the noisy engine.

The nearest woman leapt over a low hedge, caught her left sandal in the shrubbery, and flew face first into the grass. Her face came to rest on a light designed to cast a purple shadow on the shrubbery for passing night motorists. The woman's face twisted it off and cables trailed after her as she skidded to a halt.

'That's got to hurt,' laughed Imo, exiting after Jason. 'Stay in here. Don't open the doors for anyone,' warned Imo to the woman beside her. As she clambered down the ladder Jason had left for her, she locked the door with the key fob and pocketed it. Taking the ladder away, she leant it against the nearest planter. Its top rung shaking against the thick branches and leaves of the evergreen tree within.

Turning to Jason, she failed to see a figure leap out from behind the wide foliage. The woman's green polo shirt had blood stains. Her alert red eyes bore down on Imo as she landed against her back, knocking her to the ground. 'Sabre!' Imo shouted as she struggled free.

Barking against the glass of the passenger side, Sabre pushed against the door, forcing the Eve with the memory loss to scramble to the driver's seat and cower.

Fumbling for her cleaver, Imo watched as Jason swiftly felt for the hilt of his combat knife and thrust it at the woman's throat. With a two-handed grip, he pushed as hard as he could, twisted against the soft cartilage of her oesophagus and withdrew his blade. A hard crunching noise accompanied his movements. As the woman fell to the ground, Jason rushed to the other planter, stooped by the roots, and vomited.

'Nice kill!' marvelled Imo, watching the flow of blood. 'Shame to waste it. Sabre must be hungry.'

At this comment, Jason dry heaved into the planter, stood up and hoarsely spoke into his mic, 'One enemy neutralised, sir.'

'Well done, Flight Sergeant Harper. What do you want, a medal?'

Imo stood up straight, eyes wide, beaming, showing one of her stumpy teeth through her semi-open lips. 'We getting medals? Cool, that'll look good on my uniform.' She smoothed down her combat shirt, brushing past the bulging pouches of her webbing. Puffing her chest out, 'Will there be a ceremony and a parade?' Looking at her muddy boots, splattered with dried blood, 'Hey, Cowboy, you'll have to show me how to get my boots shiny.'

'Get a grip,' crowed the colonel. 'No one is getting a medal.'

Whispering, 'I doubt we'll get out of Aberdeenshire, Imo. This mission will last until we've eradicated all the infected. I'll never see Pippa again. We've committed so many atrocities.' Dropping his knife, he fell to his knees and wept.

Spotting the fallen Eve rise from the grass, Imo lifted his knife and thumped Jason on his shoulder. 'The colonel is right. Get a grip. We have almost cleared this area. We'll be at the fence soon. There is always hope.' Into her mic, she asked, 'Where is the next heat source?'

'Well, you've got some running at you, but the one I want is in the garden centre. To the left. Bring them all alive,' hissed the colonel. 'I know two heat sources have gone cold.'

Chapter 34

Pushing aside abandoned shopping trolleys, Jason and Imo pulled apart the internal sliding doors. The colonel hadn't turned the electrics on for this building. The body that was jammed between them tumbled to the floor, its exposed spine wobbling. Bones scattering like a game of skittles as the upper torso went one way and the legs and abdomen fell the other way. Rancid bowels spilling onto the linoleum, slipping like live eels. 'Can't make up his mind whether to shop or not!' exclaimed Imo, watching Jason dry heave.

They struggled through the gap, Imo catching her stuffed pouches on the glass door. Cursing, she wedged through, stepping over the entrails. Twisting, she caught sight of Adam's drugged disciples wandering around the vehicle. She could hear Sabre's barking.

Staring up at the wall of jigsaw, tartan scarfs, perfume, tinned fudge, and Scottish tablet sweets, Jason pointed. 'It's like a maze. We'll have to follow the shopping experience path.'

Handing him his combat knife, 'I hate these types of shops. You can't get out quick.'

Grinning, holding the knife in the classic combat pose, 'Not good for shoplifters?'

Pocketing a tin of mints and a necklace, she winked at him. 'I'll have to teach you some moves. If we ever get a minute to ourselves.'

Nodding to her pockets and pouches, 'You should empty them. Then you wouldn't get stuck in doors.'

Snapping their heads forward at the sound of a scraping chair, inching forward, one behind the other. Imo turning around every few steps to make sure none of the women were following them in. Turning back in time to see Jason's hand signals, she gave him a thumbs up, ignored him, and went sprinting forward, meat cleaver raised. Running forward with a yell, she bumped into a display of Nordic socks blocking her path. Rows of their thick fabric cushioning her fall.

Sniggering, Jason took the lead, turning left at the scattered display. Hearing Imo curse and rise to her feet, he scanned the room, taking in the café chairs, tables, and long counter. Cakes, sandwiches, panini, and other baked goods had festered over the weeks since the attack. Green mould flourished, the stench overpowering the fruity aromas from the nearby candles in large jars. Bodies laid on the floor. Some were bent over tables and between the cake cloches on the counter, as if closely examining ingredients and baking techniques. They were decomposing, appearing to move, the maggots within eating through to the muscles and tendons. Jason gagged, wishing he could slip on a respirator with a filter.

Nudging past him, Imo raised her cleaver, making to lob it at the man, wandering with a tray of mouldy sandwiches, flies buzzing around it and him. Two cups, two saucers and a teapot were rolling around the tray.

Jason snapped his hand forward, grabbing her wrist, halting her throw.

'He's clearly infected,' she hissed, struggling with him. 'This isn't normal behaviour.'

'Look carefully,' he warned, keeping his grip tight.

Relaxing her arm, Imo allowed Jason to keep a check on her while she settled her sight more closely on the man. Squinting her eyes, she saw his trousers were urine stained and when he turned to sit at the table; there were brown stains on the seat of his trousers. When the man rose again and returned to the counter, she realised that what she mistook for blood around his mouth was a different shade. It looked like he'd been snacking on beetroot. Looking at the nearby fridge, realisation dawned on her when she spotted the cherry flavoured drinks.

Jason let go of her wrist.

'Why hasn't he seen us?' asked Imo, baulking as the man raised a maggot-ridden sandwich to his lips.

Rushing over, Jason gently took the sandwich from the man, smiling at his frowning face.

He had thinning grey hair, in need of a good brush. Dandruff covered his shoulders. The deep lines on his forehead and around his eyes spoke of a life lived long. His neck strained, looking like a tortoise. Croaking, as if not used to speaking, the man rose stiffly. 'Well Jack, is it shift time already? I haven't had time to eat my sandwich. Our break times are never long enough. Oh, well, back to the factory floor it is.'

'The fuck is he on about? He's a pork pie short of a picnic,' quipped Imo, wandering around, bending at corpses, pushing her hand down in her pouches.

Keeping his face agreeable despite the stench of urine and faeces, Jason nodded. 'That's right pal, time to go.' He beckoned the man with his hand.

Rising, the man frowned as his gaze settled on an elderly lady laid out under the seat opposite him. Half of her face was missing, and flies were feasting within the green flesh.

Whispering, Jason pointed at the ceiling and windows. 'The heat from the glass all around will have advanced decomposition. This is the worst. Things are only going to get ghastlier, Imo. I hope the colonel issues us some respirators or face masks with decent filters.'

Their comms remained silent, and Imo and Jason shrugged at each other.

Imo wrinkled her nose. 'He needs a good shower.' Gingerly lifting thumb and index finger, she dipped into his back pocket and withdrew his wallet. 'His name is Lewis.' Slipping the wallet back into his pocket, she stepped back.

'Not going to take his money?'

Winking, then wrinkling her nose again, 'I've standards, you know. I never handle dirty money.'

Joining her, relieved at not having to kill, he quipped, 'Not experienced in money laundering?'

'Ha! Nice one.' She high-fived him, their hand slapping, startling the man.

'Where's Betty?' asked Lewis, looking around him.

Jason quickly took him by the shoulders, walking him away to the café exit, through another section of the shopping maze. As he passed displays, he picked up two towels, a tartan apron, some thin waterproof gardening gloves, and some perfumed liquid soap. 'We'll go find her, Lewis.'

Imo lifted the chair from Betty's corpse. 'She's here, Jason. Not that he'll want to see her. I don't think you do, either.' She feigned gagging.

'I'll clean him up as best as I can in the accessible toilet. Have a look around and see if you can find any clean clothes that'll fit him. Go along with what he says. Live in the moment with him. I think he has dementia. I doubt he even realised he was eating rancid food. Poor bloke.' Jason continued to walk with Lewis and turned into the small corridor housing the toilets.

Shrugging her shoulders, Imo lifted Betty's purse, rifled through it, wrinkling her nose, and dropped it. Turning, she glanced at the rotting men's corpses. 'Fucked if I'm stripping you naked for your clothes.' Following the next path of the shopping maze, heading for what she hoped would be the men's section of jackets, she pulled down a pink silk pashmina, bunching it up. Walking past the toilet area, she strolled past the books like an absent-minded shopper and her glazed eyes lit up when she saw the dog food section. Grabbing the nearest trolley, pushing off a dead child hanging from a strap, she left it dangling like a teether on a ribbon, swinging. Pushing the trolley towards the gigantic bags of dog biscuits, she tutted as the child's body bounced against her knee. Slicing through the straps with her cleaver, she stepped over it as it bounced on the floor, landing by the bird fat ball boxes. Imo filled her trolley with treats for Sabre, wishing her companion was by her feet, running around free to feast. Her fingers idly floated in the air, as if stroking her best friend.

Rushing past the cat section, Imo grabbed at a pair of waterproof trousers with an elastic waistband and a wax jacket.

Jason, dressed in an apron and bright yellow gloves, opened the door of the toilet.

Shrugging, Imo passed him the jacket and trousers but thought better of the pashmina. 'That's the best I can do. The corpses are too far gone. No one would want to wear their clothes.'

'Thank you, Imo. I've cleaned Lewis up as best as I can. This'll keep his modesty until we get him to the fence. He still thinks he's at work.'

Watching the door close, Imo wondered what type of factory had strangers stripping and washing you. She wheeled her trolley back to the door, standing clear of it, watching the women tire themselves out, running around the monster truck. Sabre had given up barking and Imo watched with jealousy as the woman with the missing memory was stroking him and fussing over him.

'Green-eyed monster?' rejoined Jason.

'No,' snapped Imo. Muttering, 'He's my dog.'

Rolling his eyes at the contents of the trolley in front of her, 'You spoil him.'

Winking, she retorted, 'Green-eyed monster, much?'

Chapter 35

The other Eves were panting as they sat against the thick monster truck's tyres. Each with frowning foreheads as if they were taking an exam and were reading a tough question. The older rose to her feet as Jason and Imo approached with Lewis.

'Where are we? This place seems familiar. Why is the army here?'

Tutting, Jason growled, 'Why does everyone think this is an army uniform? Do they expect us Royal Air Force personnel to be wearing flight suits?'

Laughing, Imo upended the nearest trolley, sprung up and opened the door to the truck. A wet tongue ran the length of her chin to forehead. Giggling, 'Wait till you see what I've got for you, boy!' Turning, 'Eve one. Pass us those bags.'

Seeing the pointing finger, the younger woman rose, looking constantly around, and hefted up the first bag. Her mouth opening and closing as if about to ask questions but thought better. Seeing the other woman in the cabin, she exclaimed, 'I know you, don't I?'

'It's like a convention. Happy reunion,' mocked Imo, slitting the bag open with her cleaver and throwing biscuits into the seats behind her.

Sabre darted back, squeezing through the gap, paws landing on a comatose Adam, squeezing a groan from him.

Screaming, the other Eve put her hand to her mouth and pointed at Adam.

'I know. The team-up is complete.' Shoving her with the sole of her boot, she ordered, 'Just get in the back. I don't have time for explanations. You'll get your free counselling in Dundee.' Pushing the woman through, watching she didn't tread on Sabre's paws. Turning to see Lewis extend his arm, Imo glanced at Jason. 'Is he definitely shit and piss clean? I'm not having him stink my cabin out.'

Grabbing her cleaver, wrestling it from her grip, Jason shouted, 'You don't have an option.' He pushed Lewis into the cabin and slammed home the door. Jumping down, he landed by the last of the Eves, pushing her head down. 'Keep still, stay there,' he hissed.

Running past the planters, Jason sprinted to the far car park. A figure wearing a lime green polo shirt and the embroidered insignia of the garden centre was sprinting towards him. He carried a garden fork, held out like a rifle with bayonet fixed. His eyes were red and firmly staring at Jason with hunger. He was yelling incoherently.

Ignoring the metallic slam of the truck door and running steps behind him, Jason thrust his arm back. Still sprinting, his arm whipped forward, and the cleaver flew through the air. It embedded itself between the infected man's eyes, splitting open his skull. A torrent of blood gushed from the hewn flesh, washing down his eyes, nose, and chin. The man fell face first, pushing the blade further back into his skull with the sound like a lumberjack at the chopping block.

Running to the nearest planter, Jason heaved amongst the roots.

'That's one way to fertilise the plants,' joked Imo. Slapping him between the shoulders. Snarling, 'Why do you always have to have the fun with my new weapons?'

Before he could wipe his mouth and retort, their comms burst through. 'Wrong report. It was time-stamped a few hours ago. Our recent drone sweep says your area is now secure. No other heat sources. Find vehicles for the survivors and direct them to the fence.'

Looking in the air, Imo snarled, 'No apology? Your incompetence could get us killed. You're a fuckwit!'

Standing up from the planter, Jason shrugged at Imo. 'Sir, the civilians are in no fit state to drive. Adam drugged them.' Hesitating, 'He has been injured during the rescue.'

Imo smirked, winking at Jason.

Continuing, Jason explained to the colonel. 'We also have a man who has what I think is dementia.'

'You're a fucking doctor, now,' snarled the colonel.

Jason winced at the sudden volume in his ear. 'I had a relative with the condition, sir. He is confused and cannot drive. The man we rescued will have to be taken to the fence, sir, along with the women as passengers.'

'How very convenient,' mocked the colonel. 'It'll be a drop off. Then back to your mission.'

'No, dickhead,' interrupted Imo. 'Jason will see his wife. No phone calls. In person.' Breaking off for a second, 'And I would like a shower and a hot meal. Freshly cooked. Chicken nuggets, chips, and sweetcorn on those skewer things. A cold drink, no, make that two cold cans of fizzy orange. Ice cold. And a whole lemon cheesecake. None of that shop bought shit. The same meal for Jason, after he's seen his wife. Unless she can tell your chef what his favourite meal is. And fresh meat for Sabre. Plenty of it. Liver, beef, chicken, the full works.'

'Denied,' came the immediate answer. 'Drop off only. I shall re-arm you. The mission stays the same.' The comms went dead.

'Sorry about your cleaver,' muttered Jason, turning back to the truck, slouching off.

Staring at the corpse, 'I'd like to bury something between that colonel's eyes. One day I will.' Imo strode off after Jason, the truck's ignition key coming out of her pocket.

Chapter 36

Screaming from behind her caused Imo to wince. Staring in her mirror, 'Shut the fuck up! If you don't like the view, close your eyes.'

Nodding in satisfaction, Imo glanced at the corpses and body parts they were passing. Swerving around the crater, not caring that it threw the women behind her around. 'He's waking up!' one shrieked.

Twisting around, Jason failed to notice the older Eve had her hands under the blanket that was keeping Adam warm. 'All is well, Lewis. We'll soon have you somewhere safe where you can shower and have a meal.'

'With Betty?' Lewis asked eagerly.

'Tell us about Betty?' encouraged Jason.

Lewis talked, though no one could hear his soft-spoken words above the groaning coming from Adam.

'I broke the fucker's jaw,' complained Imo, turning left at the traffic lights. 'You'd think we'd get peace from the nonsense he was spouting. I bet he's still trying to preach, claiming he is the first of the new human race.'

Turning back and shrugging, Jason placated her with, 'They'll soon be off our hands.' Looking wistful, he whispered, 'But what, then, for us?'

Imo slowed the vehicle as they returned to the King George V Park. A smouldering Guide hut was giving off the odd puff of smoke, like an exhausted dragon. It had collapsed in on itself and was a pile of burn-out wood.

Jason pointed to their Land Rover. 'Back to say goodbye to the old girl? The colonel will re-supply us. New weapons will be clean and oiled, better for preventing stoppages. We both need pistols and I'm sure we'll get new rifles and a shotgun for you.' He remembered about the Mills bombs. 'Unless Ukraine has them all and the UK supplies have run out.'

'It's not that,' replied Imo, stroking Sabre, who was taking up most of the passenger seat. Jason found himself squashed against the window again.

'Ah!' Light dawned on Jason and a cheeky grin spread across his face. 'Your stash is in there.'

Showing Jason her toothless mouth, Imo returned the grin. 'Yes. That as well. This truck isn't good for my lad here. He can't scrabble up.' Drawing Sabre nearer for a cuddle, 'He's going to hurt himself one day, jumping out of this height.'

'True. Okay. You go ahead to the fence. Your enormous wheels can clear a path for us. Our passengers will be safer in this truck. I'll be right behind you in the Land Rover. It'll be best if we don't take on any of the infected.' He patted his empty holster and ammunition pouch. Shouting over his shoulder, 'Keep strapped in. It could get bumpy.' Pointing to the open tailgate of the Land Rover, 'Park alongside, I can jump onto that.'

Imo manoeuvred around the debris strewn car park and eased alongside their Land Rover. Craning her neck around Sabre, keeping a tight hold of him as she eyed up her stash of stolen goods wedged between two of the military kit-bags, she sighed in relief. Once she saw Jason leap from the tailgate and make his way to the driver's seat, she pulled the truck away and drove it in front of the Land Rover. She idled the engine, enjoying hearing its roar. Imo failed to notice the door to her left ease open and didn't hear Sabre's growls. Pulling him towards her, she shouted, 'That roar is deeper than your barks, boy!' Laughing, she checked her mirror and squinted. Jason was waving and then pointing.

Ahead of her, a figure in a crimson stained white robe ran to the car park exit, a woman in a mauve dress following. They stopped, blocking the exit. The woman stood about a foot from a wall while Adam was dead centre, arm raised ahead, palm out. His open jaw sagged; pain etched deep within the lines of his forehead. Incomprehensible sounds broke through each settling rumble from the truck's engine.

Smirking, Imo gunned the motor again, this time pulling off the handbrake, accelerating hard. Ignoring the cries of, 'Watch out!' coming from one of the Eves behind her. She bore down on Adam.

Jason watched in shock as he rocked his head and cried, 'No, Imo, no.' Starting the Land Rover's engine and feeling relieved that it worked immediately. He sat open-mouthed.

Screaming another rebel yell, Imo pushed down hard on the accelerator. Seeing Adam raise both hands high in the air, as if in surrender, she laughed. 'That's right, dickhead. Time to go to heaven.'

The truck lurched to the right as Adam disappeared under one enormous wheel. The sound of his crunching bones, squelching flesh and splattering blood was silenced as the engine roared in triumph. What remained of him was pulverised to a pulp under the rear left side tyre.

Jason gulped hard as he drove forward and saw the remains looking like something that would have gone on a topping of the pizza takeaway on the High Street. Driving to the screaming Eve, he inadvertently drove over Adam's heart, mashing it. Seeing her fingernails clawing at the glass of the passenger window and the spittle flying as she shrieked at him, Jason shouted, 'Forget it. You are on your own. You've made your choice.' He drove off after the monster truck that had swerved to its left and sped off past the Scout hut. He hoped the teenagers and their leader had got to the fence safely. Muttering to himself, 'Pippa had better be there. I need her. God, do I need to see her after all this?'

Chapter 37

Imo laughed joyfully as she crunched down on the decaying bodies dispersed around the roads leading out of Banchory. She took delight in mangling a fallen moped driver's body, his insulated box's lid flapping in the wind as she bore down on him. 'That's for delivering cold pizza!' she quipped, nudging her left elbow. Her face fell as she remembered Jason wasn't beside her. Checking in her mirror as the truck lurched, then settling, she was relieved to see Jason following her. Her shouts and threats of violence against them had kept the surviving Eves quiet. She could see they were busy pacifying a confused Lewis.

Rising over a crushed car, like a battlefield tank, Imo yelled another ululation, hoping Jason could wedge the Land Rover through the wreckage.

The two vehicles, looking incongruous in size, steered onto the A90. It was barren. Imo's eyes raised in surprise. Then she swore when she saw there was no more fun to be had from mutilating corpses or crushing cars. Instead, she gunned the engine, watching the speedometer rise, leaving Jason to plod along behind her.

The watchtowers along the fence appeared as small structures, like distant transmission towers. Within a few seconds, they appeared to bear down on the surrounding farmland like they were on a silent vigil. Imo eased off the accelerator and allowed the truck to coast along, its sped gradually lessening. Stepping softly on the brake, she stared ahead and saw the new structures, like office towers. They had built the Portakabins upon each other, like a giant was playing a game of Tetris. A series of metal stairs and bannisters on the side had been bolted on, like an afterthought. She watched as figures scurried up and down, entering and departing doors in a rush. Recognising the muzzle of the GPMGs and sniper rifles poking from each watchtower, she kept a running commentary to Jason of the armaments she saw. As she approached the double-fenced area, she wondered if it had got taller. The no-man's-land remained as barren, but through the second gates she saw a series of single Portakabins. One was painted white with a red cross in its centre. A familiar figure was pacing across the width of the gate in the first fence. Behind him were figures in combat uniform, kneeling or standing, each with a rifle raised.

As the roar of the monster truck's engine subsided, the sound of a low-flying helicopter superseded it. It swooped over them and lowered itself behind the series of Portakabins, then fell out of sight. Its rotor blades noise falling to a gentle thrum.

Imo stuck her right hand out of her window and with her palm facing the tarmac, she lowered it, raised it gently and lowered it again, like she was imitating flying.

Behind her, Jason understood her actions and pulled alongside her, reversing so the tailgate of the Land Rover backed into the driver's door of the truck. He left space for the door to open.

Imo jumped across the gap, whistling for Sabre. She thrust her hand out to the nearest Eve.

Running from the Land Rover, not bothering to turn off the ignition or close the door, Jason screamed, 'Pippa!' repeatedly. Bashing into the gate, face bunched into the gaps of its metalwork, he looked across the length of no-man's-land. Scanning the breadth of what he could see of the Angus County, narrowing down on the gate beyond and its immediate surroundings. His shoulders slumped when he saw only military figures. None looked pleased to see him.

Striding over, the second gate locking behind him, the colonel shouted, 'She's not here, Flight Sergeant.' Laughing, 'I said I denied your request.' Watching in delight as Jason fell to his knees, hands reaching through the gaps in the gate.

The colonel flicked his head to the side of the gate. 'Hand over the hostages, then pick up those kit-bags and ammunition boxes and fuck off to the grid reference circled on the map. I doubt you'll find him. Well, not alive anyway. But it'll please the politicians.' He unlocked the gate.

'Who the fuck you talking about now? Another of your undercover operatives?' snarled Imo, hoisting Jason onto his feet. 'Another sneaky-beaky?' Winking at the colonel, 'Want us to bring his festering body back?'

Winking back, opening the gate. 'Yes! You are so going to love this mission. No spoilers!'

'Nice to see you, too, dickhead. You are never going to let us through these fences? Are you?' Imo whistled for Sabre and pointed to her heel. The dog ran over and sat by her.

Two burly men, dressed in combat fatigues and beige berets, each holding a long, thin, paddle-like gadget, like the scanners at airports, stepped forward.

'Drop your combat knives. You can pick them up on the way out. I'll spoil you today. Step into no-man's-land. Don't worry, it's not mined. Yet.' The colonel stepped back. 'Don't forget, we have snipers and gunners in the watchtowers. They are just itching for you to give them an excuse.' Nodding curtly to the two men, 'Scan them.'

Limping forward, like they had a leg shorter than the other, the men broke off and each paired up with either Jason or Imo. They ran their scanners over the arms, legs, and torso of Jason and Imo. The man scanning Jason had no left hand. A heavily bandaged stump poked out from his cuff.

A sharp buzzing noise erupted angrily from the machine scanning Imo, and the guard's fingers danced in the air. He eyed Sabre warily.

Imo tutted as she dropped her knuckle-duster. 'That better still be here when I come back,' she hissed.

Running his scanner over her other leg, the gadget buzzed until Imo dropped a handful of ball bearings.

'Don't worry, Poacher, there are several boxes in the kit-bags. It would be a shame not to see your catapult in action. It so pleases my camera operators.' The colonel pointed to the Portakabins.

'You can see everything we do, sir?' asked Jason.

'Oh, yes,' grinned the colonel. 'And we record. From the sky, buildings, roofs, lampposts, shops, oh, so many ways.'

Jason looked down at his boots as the guard finished scanning him.

Shaking his head, the colonel taunted, 'So many war crimes. Where do I begin?'

'With me, dickhead,' hissed Imo above the noise of the buzzing. 'Leave Jason out of this.'

The guard's scanner was going into overdrive as it ran up and down Imo's bulging pouches.

Slipping off her webbing belt, she snarled, 'This better not go missing this time.' She pondered about asking Sabre to guard it.

The colonel waved his hands in the air. 'Let her have her spoils of war.'

Imo grinned and ushered the guard away with a shake of her hand. She watched him limp off, seeing the loose fabric of his combat trousers around his left leg flap about.

The guards stood behind their colonel; scanners pushed into their trouser pockets. One hand resting on their pistol grips secured in their holsters.

'Tell your survivors to come out and go through the second gate. Say your sweet goodbyes.'

Staring over, Jason was relieved to see a man wearing a blue v neck scrub top and matching trousers. His white trainers looked out of place amongst the boot wearing soldiers. Lewis would be in the hands of caring nurses now.

'Glad to get rid of them,' moaned Imo. 'They are all away with the fairies.'

'And Adam is back with his creator,' mocked the colonel.

Grinning, Imo watched as the Eves helped Lewis walk through the grassy area and beyond the second gate. None looked back or said goodbye.

Shouting at them, Imo sneered, 'A thank you wouldn't have hurt.'

'Not many survivors for two day's work,' jeered the colonel.

'We saved the Scouts.' Jason pointed at the stack of bicycles leaning against the first set of Portakabins.

'Yes, you are ingenious with your modes of transport, Poacher.' Grinning at the truck. 'Leave the keys in the ignition. I've promised my troops some recreation time with it.'

'We need that, sir. The recreation time, I mean.' Standing on tiptoe, Jason strained to look around the second gated area.

'Denied,' jeered the colonel. 'Turn around and start your next mission. Like I said, the map is in the kit-bag, along with what armaments we can spare.' Turning to Imo, 'The hammer was a nice touch. Literally!'

Imo beamed, curtsied, and stared at the nearest camera. 'You're welcome!'

'Right. Fuck off!' ordered the colonel.

Stepping forward, Imo reached into her jacket pocket. 'I have something for you, Colonel.'

Chapter 38

Frowning, the colonel raised an eyebrow in expectation. As quick as a flash, Imo whipped out her empty hand, clenched it, and punched him full in the face.

The colonel's head whipped back; blood pouring from his nostrils. He blew each nostril with a finger while waving his men back. Blood seeped into his mouth, and he spat this out as he ordered, 'Leave her. She is mine. The bitch is mine.'

Roaring, running at him, Imo screamed, 'I am no one's bitch.' Jumping, striking out her leg straight in the air, her booted foot aimed at the colonel's stomach.

Catching her foot, he twisted it violently, forcing her to spin and fall to the ground. Releasing her as she fell hard, he punched her shin, then her thigh, and then full in the groin as he made his way up her body. He sprang on her.

Howling in pain and rage, Imo struggled against the weight pinning her down. Jabbing with her fingers, she poked one in the corner of his eye. She pushed hard, delighting in his howl.

Blinded on one side, the colonel head butted her, striking a glancing blow to her temple.

Crying out, Imo clawed in a daze, scratching down the side of his face. Digging deep, her short nails gouging a narrow tract until she reached his mouth, and he bit down. Snatching away her fingers, she bunched them into a fist and pummelled his cheek until she felt him move slightly. She lay back, exhausted, the colonel still on top of her.

Laughing, he slapped her repeatedly, cackling with each backhanded stroke. 'You are my bitch,' he yelled with each humiliating strike. Leaning back, sitting astride her, he jeered as she struggled between his knees, pinning her to the grass.

Grinning, she relaxed and stroked his thighs, reaching down, caressing his shins. 'Yes, Colonel Winters,' she said submissively.

With leering mouth exposed, the colonel flashed her his bright white teeth, licking his lips and reaching forward to kiss Imo.

Quickly unbuttoning her trouser leg pocket, Imo whipped out a weapon she'd squirrelled away during her first delve into a kit-bag. Pulling out the short, but thick, solid wooden truncheon-like trench club, winking as she rammed it into the colonel's jaw. Teeth shattered as this relic from the First World War drove through his mouth, stopping as it hit the roof of his open mouth. It looked like he was performing fellatio on it. Imo thrust it up and down like an eager lover, smashing more of the colonel's teeth, splitting open his gums. Laughing, she sprang up, pushing him off her. Jumping on his prone figure, clasping his neck, and leaning in as if to give him a love bite. Instead, she bent over his ear and whispered, 'I'm no one's bitch. Dickhead.' Drawing back her short club, she made to clobber him with it when a female voice demanded, 'That's enough!'

Chapter 39

Striding over to Imo was a woman in a grey-blue skirt, barely black hosiery, and a service single-breasted jacket. Rows of gold braid circled her lower sleeves, with more gold stretching from her right shoulder to a belt-like sash around her waist. Its tassels bouncing with each stride. Rows of colourful ribbons lined her left breast. Above them, she wore an aircrew flying badge wings with a crown above the RAF lettering. The gold decoration continued on her rank epaulettes.

The guards stood to attention and saluted.

Twisting, seeing all the adornments on the uniform, Imo quipped, 'You look important.'

'Ah, Imo, I was told you had a sharp tongue. Please drop the club.'

'No. I'm keeping this bad boy.' Pocketing it, she pointed at the crying colonel. Showing her toothless grin, Imo boasted, 'Look what it did. Now he looks like me!'

'Indeed,' replied the woman, stretching her arm out.

Imo took it and was helped to her feet. Tightening her grip, the woman pumped her hand up and down twice. 'Air Commodore Joanna Thorn. Pleased to meet you, Imo. Thank you for all you have done for our country.' Releasing her grip, turning to Jason, she failed to see Imo's jaw drop. Air Commodore Thorn saluted Jason. 'Flight Sergeant Harper, you are a credit to your uniform and the Royal Air Force. Thank you. Not a straightforward job. Most unique.'

Eyes wide, Jason stood ramrod straight and returned the salute, stammering, 'Thank you, ma'am.'

Rising swiftly, pushing between the duo, the colonel spat out a broken, bloody tooth. 'He's a war criminal, ma'am. She's worse. Arrest them both. I've plenty of evidence.'

With a curled lip, Air Commodore Thorn sneered at him. 'Don't be a prick, Colonel. The rules of engagement have been fluid. I have negotiated this with COBRA. As a matter of fact, I have flown back from a meeting with our Parliament's finest. I have their blessing.' Turning to the man with one hand, 'Sergeant, arrest Colonel Winters. Use your gadget, scan, and disarm him first.' Glancing at Imo, 'And do it properly, this time, or I'll have you demoted. There are two military police officers by my helicopter who will be delighted to receive him.'

'You can't be serious,' spluttered the colonel, his eye twitching. He spat another fragment of tooth onto the grass.

'You can't be serious, ma'am, is what I think you mean.' Winking at Imo, 'I think Colonel Winters may need some encouragement, young lady.'

Grinning, Imo stepped forward, reaching in for her trench club.

Sprinting to the far-off gate, the colonel didn't look back.

'Gentlemen, you have given a leg in the service of your country. I do not expect you to run after that poor excuse for an officer, though I know we have gifted you the best of artificial legs through the Help for Heroes mobility fund. Please be dismissed. I know my military police will be ready to apprehend him.'

Jason, eyeing up the opened far gate. 'Ma'am, you mentioned the Rules of Engagement?'

'Have no fear, Flight Sergeant Harper. You and Imo are free from any prosecution. I will wipe all data that Colonel Winters has collected. Our surveillance will continue, but only to ensure your safety and to work with you. As you know, there is no cure for this chemical weapon. The infected and anyone who hampers your duty in killing the infected are considered war combatants. I see no war crimes, nor do I envisage any occurring.' Seeing Jason's slumping shoulders and sigh of relief, she continued. 'I am sorry. We need you both to continue in this mission. We are short of personnel.

I even had to fly my helicopter here. UK based personnel has been reduced to those wounded or in the Reserve but not fit for active service. The conflicts in Ukraine and the Middle East have kept us busy.' Pursing her lips. 'I blame the same politicians I've met today. Their defence cuts were harsh.'

'We need more weapons,' demanded Imo, rubbing at her red face, wishing she could have struck again for all the slapping the colonel humiliated her with.

Laughing, the Air Commodore replied with, 'You are very creative in finding your own weapons. Keep it up! But I see your need.' Stooping to tickle Sabre's ear, 'He's a lovely dog, I'm glad you found each other. I will replenish your Land Rover. As you can imagine, our stocks are low. Armament factories are in full production, like they were in my grandfather's day. You are not the only team operating in Aberdeenshire. It is a big county and there is the heavily populated city as well. Not all of them make it back to the fence.'

Jason's eyebrows arched. 'I wondered if that might be the case.' He let out another sigh of relief. His thoughts returned to his unborn baby. *Perhaps I'll be there for the birth*, he thought.

The gates enclosing Aberdeenshire were being closed by two female corporals. One had a metal claw for a hand. She deftly used this to slide through a large bolt. Metal on metal sounded out across the fields.

Looking down at her highly polished shoes, which had a splattering of mud reaching up to her hosiery, the Air Commodore lifted a leg. 'I'm not in the best attire. I did not want to miss seeing you. My Flight Sergeant in the HQ beyond the fence made it clear I needed to remove Colonel Winters today. It will be an hour before your Land Rover is serviced and loaded. Time for a hot shower and a change of uniform.' Handing over Imo a cloth badge with two crossed rifles, she grinned when she saw Imo's beaming smile. 'You've earned this, Imo. Well done.'

Grabbing it, holding it down for Sabre to sniff, then nudging Jason elbow to elbow. 'I got one, Cowboy! How about that!' Placing it on her uniform sleeve, she twisted about, showing it off.

Looking straight at Jason, smile gone, the Air Commodore continued. 'Your next mission's target is top priority. Has been since day one. No team has made it back. But he has waited this long, and I doubt he is still alive. Still, got to keep the politicians happy and complete the mission. One hour won't make much difference. You can clear the village while you hunt for him, or his body. I have someone who has been longing to see you, Flight Sergeant. Well, two, really.' Standing aside, the Air Commodore smiled and turned to Imo. 'Let's have a chat over coffee. Bring Sabre, I've a special meal waiting for him, and you.'

Jason could see the second fence and surrounding Portakabins much clearer now his superior officer had moved aside. There, by the gate, waving frantically, was a familiar figure to him. Only her abdomen was now much more extended, forcing her jacket buttons to almost pop. Jason ran.

Chapter 40

Slipping in the grass, Jason picked himself up and sprinted across no-man's-land like a combatant seeking a foxhole. He rushed through the open gate, ignoring the corporal who was holding its thick padlock. Flashing past him, he narrowed the gap between him and the waving woman. 'Pippa!' he screamed, crying, snot flowing from his nostrils, tears blinding him. Running into her arms, he embraced her, holding on tight, bending backwards so he wouldn't squash their baby. 'I love you!' he repeated through sobs. He felt her warmth and then movement as she rocked him. Their tears fell on each other's shoulders. Her slender fingers ran through his matted hair, carefully loosening knotted tangles. Another hand stroked his neck, then his dirt-encrusted face. He felt her break off the hug and take a step back.

Pippa gasped. Reaching for his face, she rubbed at his blood-smeared cheek. 'Oh, my poor baby. What have they done to you?'

'It isn't mine,' he confessed, glancing down. Eyes tightly furrowed. 'They made me kill again. I am so sorry, Pippa. I promised you and promised myself I wouldn't.'

Snatching away her hand, she rubbed her fingers on her jacket. Seeing his anguish, she regretted her actions and made soothing noises, stroking away his tears.

Between sobs, he cried out, 'I didn't want to wear the uniform. Not again. I had no alternative.'

'Air Commodore Thorn has been much kinder than that cruel colonel. She landed her helicopter on my parent's lawn.' Laughing, 'Dad was worried it would damage his beloved grass!'

Jason snorted as he gave a half laugh and half sob. 'He would!'

'Joanna explained why you had to be forced to re-enlist. She apologised for the way it happened. The colonel was a loose cannon, and she's going to ensure he gets drummed out of the military. She told me what your duties were.' Hugging him tight again, she whispered in his ear, 'I love you.' Pushing her abdomen against his, 'We love you.'

Jason collapsed, sliding out of her embrace. His face pushed against her stomach. 'I had to kill a baby!' he wailed. 'Children, so many children.'

Mouth agape, Pippa stroked the top of his head, staring, narrow eyed, to the building where they had taken the colonel. 'You must have had your reasons?' she blurted out, her tears falling onto his head.

'It was infected. They were all infected. There is no cure.'

'Joanna told me the same, before walking me to her helicopter. She was careful to strap me in the front. I was terrified. You know how much I hate heights and flying.'

'But you flew out of Aberdeen?'

'Yes, it seems so long ago. The hospital rooftop was our last hope, and it paid off, for me, at least. A sniper shot our friend. The infected were so terrifying. I thought they would kill me, rip me apart.' Tears cascaded now.

Standing, Jason wrapped his arms around Pippa. 'I thought that was what had happened. I saw his body.'

'He was feral, like an animal. Is that what you see every day?'

'Yes. So many. Imo and I must kill them before they kill any survivors.'

'You are being called a hero. By everyone I meet who knows about this operation. I've had to sign the Official Secrets Act before Joanna said anything to me. I'd have signed anything to hear about you. There has been no coverage in the news.'

Shaking his head. 'No, I don't feel like a hero. I hate what I am doing. I -'. He stopped, not wanting to confess his weakness of being sick after each kill.

Placing her hands on his cheeks, kissing him, despite the blood and mud, 'You are.'

Vigorously shaking his head, he spied Imo and the air commodore walking into a building, deep in conversation. Sabre's tail wagging as he strutted between them. Imo had put her combat webbing back on, pouches bulging.

Taking his hand, pulling him towards the building opposite the one Imo had disappeared into. 'I've people who want to meet you.'

Chapter 41

Clapping erupted from the personnel in the Ops Room as each screen operator stood up, hands working overtime, applauding for all they were worth.

Walking in, hand-in-hand with Pippa, Jason's mouth was agape as he saw the banks of screens and the number of Royal Air Force personnel. Scanning the room, his eyes settled on the senior rank, a fellow flight sergeant. Jason made his way over, not letting go of Pippa.

'Well done, Flight Sergeant,' shouted a corporal above the noise, patting Jason on the shoulder as he passed.

One screen operator was holding a wet tissue to her eyes, but was smiling at Jason and then Pippa.

Nodding to each person he passed, it surprised Jason to see them grinning at him, offering praise, and thanking him. A rush of emotion surging through him, like a shot of adrenaline from an emergency doctor. He cried some more when Pippa squeezed his hand.

Pippa stopped him, let go of his hand, reached up with a cotton embroidered handkerchief, and wiped away his tears. Her white cloth came away with scarlet streaks. She dropped it in the nearest waste bin by one desk.

Holding his arm firmly out, the flight sergeant with the freshly laundered combat uniform who oversaw the Ops Room introduced himself. Pumping Jason's hand, ignoring the dirt and blood, he grinned, then brought him in for a hug. 'Jason, it's great to finally meet you face to face. I'm Dillon Buchanan.' Breaking off the hug, looking at him directly, he pursed his lips. 'Sorry about that dick of a colonel. He's a bad one. Got a screw loose if you ask me. They should have never put him in charge of you, considering your history. You've more than made up for what happened in Yemen. You are a hero, mate.'

Holding out his right knuckle, Jason bumped it with Dillon. 'Thanks, mate,' croaked Jason.

'We've had your back. That's all you need to know about us and this room.' Pointing to the door. 'Don't waste your hour here. You can catch up with Pippa's news.' Clasping Jason firmly on the shoulder. 'The Scouts are safe, thanks to you. The pensioners from Stonehaven are thriving in their new nursing home. They've settled in nicely. Kirsty is back at university. She's even got herself a new car, much like her old one. All alive, thanks to you. Even Hazel. She volunteered straight away at the survivor's processing centre. Has promised to work around the clock, to make sure they are fed, and to talk and listen to them offload their horrors.'

Swallowing, Jason merely nodded, looking around at all the people in the room. All for him and Imo. 'Brilliant. Thanks Dillon, that's just what I needed to hear.'

'Follow me, mate. There's a hot shower waiting for you, along with a clean uniform. Then a proper home cooked meal.' Laughing, 'Imo has her chicken nuggets, but Pippa crossed out Imo's choice for you and requested other dishes from our chef.'

Dillon took them to another Portakabin. Walking around its double bed, he pointed to a sectioned off part. 'The shower room. We won't disturb you again.' Winking at Pippa, he whispered, 'Though it's too late for us to have left condoms in the bedside drawer!'

Laughing, 'You airmen all have a one-track mind.' She closed the door on Dillon, turning the lock, just in case.

'Strip!' she ordered Jason.

'Oh, love,' he said softly, 'I don't think I can. Not under these circumstances.'

Giggling, 'Not that! I want to see you clean. Now strip and get in the shower.'

Laughing, 'I've been dreaming of this moment. Of being alone with you. I've missed you.' Taking off his combat jacket and tearing off his filthy t-shirt, he heard her gasp. Looking down, turning to see his back in the mirror, he shrugged. 'Sorry about the blood.'

'It's not that. You have bruises upon bruises. What have you been through?' Seeing his fresh tears, she ordered, 'Now the other half.' Walking into the shower room, she turned the dial to a higher temperature. Checking there was shower gel and shampoo, she switched on the shower. With a high-pitched yelp, Pippa stepped back quickly to avoid getting wet.

Following her in, unabashed at his nudity, Jason stepped under the steaming water. A whirl of dirt and blood eddied at his feet before vanishing down the plughole. Lathering up, he generously applied shampoo and gel to himself.

Pippa watched him transform from a muddy beast to her beloved husband, much like he did after coming home from a six-week exercise. They'd made use of the bed on those occasions, she thought, eyes sparkling at the memories. She patted her stomach, a by-product after one such coupling.

'Oh boy!' declared Imo as she took the offered metal bowl of meat from the chef. Whistling through her stubby teeth for Sabre, she dangled a piece of chicken under his snout.

A long pink tongue snapped out, like a lizard, scoffing down the meat.

Giggling, Imo delved into the freshly cooked meat, still warm to the touch, and threw a sliver of steak at him.

Leaping up, Sabre caught it, swallowing it whole.

Placing the bowl down, watching him tear at it, nose rammed against the side of the bowl, Imo quipped, 'You'd better not have the shits later.'

The man in chequered trousers and a white tunic grinned. He pointed to a nearby table, waited for Imo to sit, then lifted a shiny silver cloche.

Imo clapped her hands like an excited schoolgirl. 'Chicken nuggets, proper chips and sweetcorn on skewers.' She eyed the nearby vinegar and large white shaker. 'Proper chip shop salt.' Grabbing a red bottle, she shook it over her meal, then did the same with the other two condiments.

Beaming, the chef walked off.

'He needs to prepare Pippa and Jason's food,' replied the Air Commodore, placing an orange fizzy drink in front of Imo. 'There's more in the fridge.' Sitting opposite Imo, she placed her hands on a china saucer and a cup of tea. A teapot nearby let off tiny puffs of steam through its spout.

Winking, chewing vigorously, Imo swallowed and grinned. 'They'll be working up an appetite.'

Smiling, the Air Commodore asked, 'Anyone special in your life.'

Imo tossed Sabre a chicken nugget. The dog ignored it and continued to chomp away at his meat. 'Just my boy, here.'

'He looks after you. Both of you. The three of you make a formidable team.' Looking stern, 'That's why I can't let you go. You must return through the fence.'

Shrugging, spiking several chips with her fork, Imo belched. 'Fine by me.'

'It doesn't bother you?'

'I've nowhere to go. No job. No money. I was about to lose my flat. What else would I do?' She mopped up the last of her red sauce with a solitary chip.

Waving her hand in the air, the Air Commodore slid Imo's plate to the side of the table. 'The killing doesn't bother you?'

'Not really. They aren't human, are they?' Imo bit her lip and lowered her voice. 'Maybe the children and the babies. But there is no alternative, is there? I always make it quick for them.'

'None. Sorry. The babies would have a horrible death. The adults and probably even the children will kill any survivors. Try to think about the living, the uninfected, I mean. You have saved so many. The Land Train out of Stonehaven was a stroke of genius. I've seen the footage. That clip will survive! So many owe you their lives. That's why I need you to go back.'

The chef arrived carrying a plate in the air. He lowered it down in front of Imo as if in slow motion. Winking at her eager face, 'Enjoy. It's a whole one. All to yourself.' Taking her empty plate, he walked off, spying Imo slip the sauce bottle into her thigh pocket where it sat side-by-side with her trench club.

Imo grabbed her spoon, glanced at Sabre, smiled when she saw him snatch a piece of liver from his bowl and swallow it whole with just two bites.

'You have feelings for him?'

Imo stared at the exiting figure and spluttered, 'Who, the chef? As if!'

Laughing, 'No. Jason.'

Imo put her spoon down with a clang. 'No.' Squinting her head. 'Not that it's any of your business, but I've been told that I'm asexual if you must know. I've been used and abused too many times. Now it's just me. And Sabre, of course. The psychologist who the court assigned me gave me that label. I had to complete a course of therapy to keep me out of prison again.'

Leaning forward, careful to keep her gold braid from falling in her tea, 'Did it help?'

'I've no idea. I was off my face half of the time!' beamed Imo.

Sliding a bottle of green liquid across, 'That reminds me, our doctor says you can take ten per cent less this week.'

Imo mumbled a thank you and slipped the bottle into an almost full pouch. Metal jingled as she settled the plastic container safely.

'Of course, we can't pay you. But in the olden days of battle, there were spoils of war. Most of our footage will not be recorded.' Grinning, 'Just your edited highlights. I might keep the trench club action for my personal pleasure. Vile man.'

Patting her pouch, 'Suits me, too.' She shovelled a huge portion of cheesecake into her mouth, crumbs of biscuit base dropping onto the table.

The outer door swung open, and Pippa and Jason strode in. Striding to Imo, Pippa declared, 'It didn't seem right for Jason to be eating without you. Sabre and you are his teammates.' As Imo stood, Pippa placed her hands around her and whispered, 'Thank you for looking after him, for keeping him alive.'

Imo broke off the embrace, curtsied, and giggled, 'You're welcome!'

Chapter 42

Staring from Pippa to Jason, Imo declared, 'You are so punching above your weight, Cowboy. Pippa is gorgeous.'

Flushing red, Pippa turned back to Jason. 'Cowboy?'

'It's a long story. Poacher here thinks she is funny.'

Twisting back to Imo, Pippa tilted her head. 'Poacher?'

'That's a short story. But what I'd like to know,' she asked as the chef balanced two cloches as he walked back, 'is what is Cowboy's favourite meal?'

'Not bacon and beans followed by coffee!' exclaimed Pippa as she fussed over Jason, directing him to sit by the Air Commodore.

Nodding, Jason sat ramrod straight. 'Ma'am.'

'Relax, Harper. Enjoy your meal. Chef has freshly prepared it.'

Pippa sat and took two plain wooden sticks from her pocket. Their base was joined to a thin strip of wood, holding them together. She placed this in front of her husband.

With a flourish, the chef lifted the cloches together to reveal square plates. A small dish of soya sauce sat on one side of each plate. Next to them was freshly rolled sushi.

Sabre's nose twitched in the air at the smell of fresh fish. His metal bowl was shiny and clean. Licked spotless.

Poking a roll of fish and rice with her spoon, Imo exclaimed, 'What the fuck is that?'

'Sushi,' answered Pippa, pushing Imo's spoon away.

'Sue what?'

'It's from Japan. It's a mixture of fish, vegetables, and rice, usually salted.'

Winking at Jason as he swallowed a piece of his meal, Imo replied, 'Oh.'

'Ignore her, Pippa. She knows full well what sushi is. She's probably done a course in prison.'

Pippa sat back in her chair. 'You went to prison?'

'Only once or twice,' grinned Imo. Laughing, 'Maybe three. But you are safe with me.'

'I know nothing about you, sorry. Where do I begin? I'd like to get to know you better.'

Jason put down his chopsticks, dabbing his mouth with his napkin. 'Probably best you don't!' he quipped. 'You wouldn't sleep again!'

Pippa gasped.

Imo reached over the table and thumped Jason on the shoulder.

Raising an eyebrow, Pippa wondered if that was the source of her husband's bruising. 'It doesn't matter. All I care about is you've kept Jason alive and now we can build a home together. You are welcome to stay with my parents as well. Until you get a new home.'

Chewing her lip, Imo replied, 'Ah. About that. I'm going back. Through the fence, back to Aberdeenshire.'

'You can't,' blurted Jason. 'You'll never survive on your own. Even with Sabre by your side.'

Turning to face him full-on, the air commodore stated, 'That's why I want you to return with her, Flight Sergeant Harper.'

Hugging her husband, Pippa shouted, 'No! I didn't agree with that. I thought the hour was for us to have Jason processed back into civilian life.' Standing, hands on her belly. 'Jason is coming with me.'

Jason rose from his chair and wrapped his hands around her. 'I failed my duty in Yemen. I must do this. For my soul. I could never look you and our child in the eye again if I walk away.'

'You've more than made up for that,' hissed Pippa, her eyes filling with tears.

'I can't leave Imo on her own. She'll get killed.'

Sitting, Pippa looked across to Imo. She saw a fragile-looking woman, full of bravado, staring back. Her gaunt features hidden below layers of dirt and other people's blood. Her shoulders sank as she realised Imo needed Jason more. 'Promise me you won't take risks. You'll keep him alive. Bring him back. Just one more mission.'

The air commodore looked away as the last sentence was said.

'I promise,' vowed Imo solemnly.

'You have a lot to discuss and the rest of your meal to finish. I'm sorry, but time is pressing. Imo, follow me. I'll show you to your shower and there are fresh clothes for you.'

'Sabre first. He needs a good shampoo and brush.'

'I've foreseen this. The shower hose will stretch to the floor. You can go in together and there is special dog shampoo and towels for you both.'

'Cool. It's like we are married too!' Rising, she tickled Sabre's ear, 'Come on, boy, let's get hot and steamy!'

Chapter 43

'I can't let you do it,' whispered Pippa as the air commodore and Imo left the room, followed by Sabre. 'I know she needs you and you are technically still in the Air Force, but we need you more.' She patted her stomach and stared at him with wet eyes.

Taking her hand, 'I can't fail in my duty, not again. The infected will rip her apart within the day. She likes to think she's a tough nut, but there is a fragile side to her. She's had no military training. I must protect her.'

'And kill again? Can you do that? Once more?'

Placing his right hand on her abdomen. 'Seeing you has given me the strength to go on, to do that. You've given me something to stay alive for. I'll return to you, I promise. I'm sure the air commodore will allow you back to see me. She is much kinder than the colonel.'

Biting the inside of her mouth, 'You are expecting to go out for more missions?' she exclaimed.

Jason nodded slowly. 'Aberdeenshire is a vast county. The population is spread out. Even trying to clear the city would take us months.'

'There must be others who can go out on missions?'

'According to the air commodore, the military is stretched. You've seen the guards with the artificial hands and legs. Not everyone makes it back, she said.'

Pippa hugged him tight. 'I know I must let you go, but you've just come back to me. While we were trapped inside the lab, the infected fought hard to get in. It was so scary. We saw what the infected did to patients and hospital staff when we ran into the basement and up the stairs to the helipad. This weaponisation of humans by the Russians is ghastly. I know you'll put them out of their misery as humanely as you can.'

Jason squeezed her tight. He didn't have the heart to tell her how much Imo enjoyed the killing. Instead, he kissed her, relishing the softness of her lips and being able to inhale her scent once again.

'That's enough of that, Cowboy! Time we hit the trail,' shouted Imo, bursting through the door. Her hair, though still wet, had a healthy sheen. She was wearing shiny new boots and combat trousers and a jacket. Patting her new badge. 'Look what I got awarded, Pippa. For being a marksman. Well, for being a markswoman. You know what I mean.'

'Well done. It is hard to achieve. Few military women attain it.' Pippa smiled weakly, taking Jason's hand.

'Thanks! The air commodore has had to go. She told me to tell you she's arranged a car and driver for you to return to your parents. She knew you weren't too comfortable flying.' Grinning her toothless smile, 'I've been promised a helicopter ride soon. I've never been on a chopper.'

'Oh, that surprises me,' replied Jason sarcastically. 'What with you being a Call of Duty veteran.'

Pippa frowned, opened her mouth, then thought better of asking. 'I hate goodbyes. Every time I saw you off on your operations and exercises, I had a heavy feeling in the pit of my stomach.'

'Now you have a bun in the oven instead!' joked Imo. Seeing Pippa's thunderous face, she added, 'Tough crowd! Jason, I'll meet you at the first gate, give you some privacy. Pippa, I'll keep my promise. Well, the one to keep Jason safe. I didn't get to keep my other to you. I didn't have a gun.'

Seeing Jason's wrinkled brow and cocked head, Pippa answered, 'I asked Imo to promise to shoot the colonel between the eyes.'

'Ha!' exclaimed Jason. 'I'd have liked to have seen that. You'll have to settle for his Court Martial instead.'

Imo leaned between them and kissed Pippa on the cheek. 'I'll watch over Jason and bring him back to you.' When she took a step back, Sabre nudged in and placed his muzzle against Pippa's stomach.

Stroking Sabre, Pippa thanked Imo, her voice breaking.

Turning away, whistling for Sabre, Imo left the Portakabin.

'I'll sit here for a while. Until you've gone. Let's say our goodbyes, Jason.'

'For now.' Kissing her on the lips. 'I'll come back soon. The air commodore mentioned it was just one village. We won't find much trouble in a village.'

'You'd better. And in one piece. Then you can tell me why I married a cowboy.'

Chapter 44

As Jason and Imo walked through the second gate, six soldiers either kneeling or standing with rifles or pistols raised flanked them. All six had at least one limb missing. Their aim was against anyone rushing through the open barrier.

'Good luck,' wished the corporal, who was missing her hand, her pistol unwavering.

'Thank you, all of you,' replied Jason as he raised his new rifle. Imo was already ahead, scanning the area with her new shotgun. They both had their pistols returned. Jason could smell that familiar aroma of gun oil. Someone had cleaned them. His pouches were bulging, like Imo's. Only his were stuffed with fully loaded magazines. His rucksack was heavily laden with cardboard boxes of fresh rounds for both weapons and cartridges for her shotgun. Flight Sergeant Buchanan had assured them that their Land Rover had been serviced and loaded with rations and enough armaments for this new mission. He had advised Jason that their orders were in the driving seat in an envelope to be opened after he'd said goodbye to Pippa. There was to be no leakage of information by a civilian, even one who had recently signed The Official Secrets Act.

Imo jumped up the tailgate of their vehicle, nodding in satisfaction when she saw the two shiny bowls for Sabre, a box labelled dog meat, and two bags of dry food. A jerrycan like container was labelled "Drinking water only" and sat alongside boxes of food for them. Delving into the first rucksack, she grinned when she saw the modern-day grenades. She took out a combat knife, its serrated edges and killing blade longer than her last. Attaching it to her belt, she patted a stack of clean blankets with cartoon dog biscuits printed on them.

Sabre jumped up, scrabbled about with his paws at the material, walked in a circle, then settled for a sleep as if he knew the length of the drive ahead.

Jumping to the grass, Imo walked around the Land Rover, her left hand casually running along its flaking and scratched paintwork. Jumping into the driver's seat, she lifted an A4 size brown envelope with Jason's full name and rank on it. She was about to rip it open when the passenger door sprang open, and Jason jumped in, snatching it from her.

Scanning through the sparkling clean windscreen and the two windows, he rested his rifle across his lap. Exhaling deeply, 'Thank you, Imo. This is my chance to make amends for Yemen.'

'You've done that already, Cowboy. Now open the envelope. I'm dying to know what fucker we've got to save. It better not be another friend of that fuckwit. If it is, I might slot him myself. Any friend of his is not a friend of mine.' Pleased with her joke, she turned to appreciate his laughter. Instead, she saw he'd turned pale. A bead of sweat broke out on his forehead and his mouth sagged open, then puckered repeatedly, like a fish as he struggled to speak.

Twisting in his seat to face Imo, Jason passed the single sheet of paper. It fluttered in his shaking hand. It had only two typed sentences. 'You'll never guess who is trapped in Aberdeenshire,' he stuttered. 'Where we are going?'

Author's Note

Ah, dear reader! I love a cliffhanger, don't you? Let me know on @CGBUSWELL where you think Jason, Imo and Sabre are going and who their mystery target is. Their adventures will return soon. In the meantime, check out my back catalogue at https://cgbuswell.com/list-books-short-stories-novels.php for your next favourite read.

Encourage my writing by leaving me a review at Amazon and/or GoodReads. It'll keep my fingers dancing on my keyboard and help with a literary contest I've entered. Part of their judging looks at the number of 5-star reviews my books receive.

I am indebted to my dear friends Ray and Katherine for their advice and eagle-eyed proofreading. If you ever need expert, remote, IT support, contact Ray at

www.crudenbaytraining.co.uk

or find him in his shop in the village Post Office.

My favourite book covers are The Fence series with their scenes of Aberdeenshire combined with the trio in action. My thanks to Amanda at Let's Get Booked for creating them and for her diligent formatting. You can see more of her talented book covers at www.letsgetbooked.com

Why not learn more about me by reading my autobiography/self-help book:

LYNNE

'A powerful account of what one dog means to one man on his road to recovery. Both heart-warming and life-affirming. Bravo Chris and Lynne. Bravo Bravehound.'
Damien Lewis, Author, and Patron of Bravehound.

Chris Buswell was brought to the brink of suicide after his son took his own life. Chris, a former army nurse, then battled military Post Traumatic Stress Disorder and anxiety. He saw no future for himself and spiralled into a deep depression. Then an assistance dog called Lynne entered his life.

Read this heart-warming tale of the bond between a Bravehound golden retriever and his army veteran.

During the unfolding of these catastrophic life events, Chris explains his self-help strategies that aided him in leading his new way of life after his bereavement and mental health diagnosis. Packed with straightforward, honest, and practical advice, you can discover easy-to-adopt-coping strategies that are simple to implement if you have PTSD and/or are grieving. He also describes his experiences with the healthcare professionals and charities who helped him get back on his feet.

Buy from
https://www.amazon.co.uk/dp/B0C3ZWQGQ4

Reviews

"I loved this book. It was heartbreaking, and funny!! Very good read as it came straight from the heart. It made you laugh and cry!! You won't want to put it down." Tracey.

"Everyone should read this book. It is honest, raw, and insightful, but with a good mix of humour. As a military vet myself and a golden retriever owner, I can relate to so much of the story. Well done for being so honest about your struggles and thank you for sharing your beautiful story." - Heather.

"A must for any veteran or nurse! Well, read your book in one go. Really interesting, honest, and raw." - Kate.

"I enjoyed reading this book even though it brought tears to my eyes! Lynn brought a smile to my face! A must read also a self-help book if you have PTSD. Great author who suffered a tragic loss." - Geraldine.

"When my mother died very unexpectedly, we donated some money to Bravehound. They allowed us to name a dog after Mum, and thankfully, Chris allowed us into a bit of his new life with my mother's namesake, Lynne.

It gives me much pride, and my sister Bernadette, to read this book. This in-depth, to the bone and very honest book gives most of us some insight into something we likely don't hear about, and thankfully, never experience. It has opened my own eyes to what our veterans experience, and the trials some have and still live through.

What a joy it is to see and hear how Lynne has helped Chris. I often feel for the 'other lady' but I'm sure she's just as much loved!

My own mother was a wonderful person, and so is Chris. Lynne has helped him achieve his potential again, and it's a privilege to read this book. The chapters are short and succinct, and the laughs and tears come quick for both sadness and joy.

Thank you for allowing us into some very dark times and for showing us that with some help, we can always find some light."

Christopher.

Also, by C.G. Buswell

Novels

The Grey Lady Ghost of the Cambridge Military Hospital: Grey and Scarlet 1

The Drummer Boy: Grey and Scarlet 2

Buried in Grief

One Last War

Group

The Fence

Zombie Haven

Dancing Unto Death

Self Help/Autobiography

Lynne: The Bravehound golden retriever dog who helped me live with my grief and military PTSD

Short Stories

Christmas at Erskine
Halloween Treat
Angelic Gift
Burnt Vengeance
The Release
Christmas Presence
Torturous Grief
Operation Wrath

Printed in Great Britain
by Amazon